The Folio Academy, over 300 strong, is writers and critics who form the unique, de facto governing body of the Rathbones Folio Prize, an annual award open to all works of literature written in English and published in the UK. With the launch of the Rathbones Folio Mentorships programme in 2017, the Academy began to undertake a more dynamic and wide-ranging role. Four members of the Folio Academy are paired with four talented students, who have taken part in First Story's in-school workshops and programmes, for a year of one-to-one talent development. Throughout the programme, which runs through the academic year, mentors and mentees meet face-to-face and online, to work on a creative writing portfolio project, which is then shared at a public showcase event.

FIRST STORY

CHANGING LIVES THROUGH WRITING

First Story is working towards a society that encourages and supports young people from all backgrounds to write creatively, for pleasure and agency. We believe there is dignity and power in being able to tell your own story, and that writing can transform lives. Our flagship programme places professional writers into schools, where they work intensively with students and teachers to develop confidence and ability. Through our core programme and extended activities, including competitions and events, we expand young people's horizons and encourage aspirations. Participants gain skills that underpin academic attainment and support achieving potential.

Find out more at firststory.org.uk.

First published 2021 by First Story Limited
44 Webber Street, Southbank, London, SE1 8QW

www.firststory.org.uk

ISBN 978-0-85748-504-5

1 3 5 7 9 10 8 6 4 2

A CIP catalogue record for this book is available from the British Library.

Printed and bound in the UK by Aquatint
Typeset by Avon DataSet Ltd
Copyedited by Alison Key
Proofread by Sally Beets
Cover designed by Julie Monks (https://julieannmonks.com)

The Day Is Fresh

An Anthology
by the Rathbones Folio Mentees

Contents

2018 COHORT

2019 COHORT

Foreword

A.L. KENNEDY

Writing is often solitary – it needs peace, concentration, that room of one's own. Talk to any successful, apparently self-made author and they will surely describe long hours of unrewarded grinding at stubborn words, perhaps multiple rejections, money worries and a weird, almost masochistic drive to keep on. Still, those same authors will talk of the people who helped: magazine editors, competition judges and, above all, other authors. Long before we reach the level where we receive professional help from literary agents, editors and the like, writers see our work, see us and see who we might become. They reach out and help. Without the help of established writers I had never met, I wouldn't be here writing this.

Under all the ego and the fretting about careers, writers suffer from an unavoidable, even inconsolable, love of good writing. The obsession that locks us into writing and rewriting pieces to completion is just as delighted by other people's pieces. As a community, we really do want good work to prosper. We're writers now, but we were readers first.

However what happens to the writers who aren't lucky? Maybe you're nowhere near a writer-in-residence or your library is closed more often than open. Maybe you can't access a local writers' group and would, anyway, be nervous to try one. Maybe you're a carer and a worker as well as a school pupil. Maybe you're studying for examinations, upon which not just your future rests, but the future of your family. Maybe the delicacy of your dreams is caught up in the pressing delicacy of your daily life. But you're a writer. You have that inconsolable love. It's there in every moment that's only yours. You are one of our family. But inside Austerity and the Hostile Environment, in post-Brexit Britain with its de-funded arts sector, with no contacts, no amiable Oxbridge tutors – what happens to you?

For a few writers, Folio Mentorships have been what happens. Following on from the wonderful work done by First Story, Folio lets people like me work with new voices as they learn their ways to sing.

The writers in this anthology are remarkable – new writers always are – but some writers have to be remarkable as human beings, just to sustain their hope enough to create. If you're puzzled about where literature or reading fit in a civilised country, or a life with meaning – it's in places like this you learn the truth of their centrality. And we need to hear the hard-pressed voices, at least as much as they need to be heard.

After decades of working with new writers, my time with Folio was simply, effectively, practically beautiful. It was a honour to spend time with my mentee and a delight to see her finally read her work in public with exactly the dignity and grace I had come to expect. She nailed it.

She will go far. She must.

In a Britain with any kind of future, every writer here must go far.

Introduction

RALF WEBB

As I write this, the fourth year of the Rathbones Folio Mentorships is coming to a close. It's a wonderful thing, that this programme has not only lasted – but thrived – over the past four years, given the well-recorded pressures on funding for the arts and, since early 2020, the lockdowns, restrictions, school closures, and individual struggles that we've all faced, and continue to face, through the pandemic. That the Mentorships have thrived is testament to each year's cohort of committed and passionate mentors, to our collaborators at First Story, and, most of all, to the mentees.

The Folio Academy Foundation is the organising charity behind the Mentorships, and up until 2017, its key activity was the Rathbones Folio Prize: an annual book prize which recognises the best book of the year, regardless of genre. The structure of the Prize is singular in this country: a huge community of over 270 writers and critics – the Folio Academy – all nominate books for the longlist and shortlist, and each year the judges are drawn from its number. But there was an ambition for the charity to be 'more than just a Prize' – to quote co-founders Andrew Kidd and Kate Harvey – 'with the unique resource of the Folio Academy being ideally placed to engage the public in exploring the power and potential of writing to transform lives.'

From this ambition, and with that simple idea at its core – that creative writing can change and transform lives – the Mentorships were founded. Each year, four members of the Folio Academy are appointed as mentors, and paired with four talented students who have taken part in First Story's creative-writing workshops and programmes in schools based in low-income communities. Across the length of a school year, the mentors meet with their mentees face-to-face and online, and work with them on a body of creative writing – from poems and short stories to novel chapters, plays, and even hybrid forms of visual and written art. At the close of the Mentorships, there is a public showcase event, where mentees read from their work to a live audience. In the first two years, this event took place in the British Library's grand Knowledge Centre auditorium – and, in the past two years, it has migrated to the virtual realm, in collaboration with Arvon: a setting that the mentees were perhaps more accustomed to than the mentors! In this anthology, we present just a taste of the creative vision and talent of many Rathbones Folio Mentorships alumni.

It is in the pairing of members of the Folio Academy and talented First Story students where this programme finds its greatest strength. I believe wholeheartedly that when you place established and emergent writers and artists together, magical things will happen – and that both parties will learn from each other, and grow through the process, through conversation, and the mutual exchange of ideas and creativity. That is what we have seen across these four years.

Any mentorship is a collaborative exercise – and so it is fitting that the Rathbones Folio Mentorships themselves, and the publication of this anthology, are the result of a fruitful and generative collaboration with First Story, one that we hope will continue for a long time to come.

The title of the anthology, *The Day Is Fresh*, is taken from a poem by Nidaa Raoof, whose work is presented here. I hope you read this book, and consider the future of creative writing and artistic expression, in the spirit of hope, brightness and optimism contained in that line.

2017 COHORT

IMARU LEWIS

Excerpt from *Ellis Friar*

Friar was much more interested in the room next to Clara's. Peering into the darkness, Friar could make out a large desk, a bookcase, several filing cabinets. So, this was an office. Friar looked for the light switch. He'd observed during the party that the brightness of the lights in this house was controlled by a dimmer switch. He risked turning the light on just slightly. It wouldn't be noticed from outside, but the visibility had already improved and Friar could see now that there was a large safe mounted on the wall on the right-hand side. He had never really got the hang of cracking safes, so avoided even trying, but the books looked valuable enough. It wasn't long before he was staggering back out onto the landing.

'Dad?' came a slurred voice. Clara's voice. Friar let out a small, pained sigh as he turned towards the voice's source. There was a shuffling and then the click of a latch as a door opened suddenly. Clara was standing there in the doorway. Friar stood motionless opposite her. No one moved. Then she asked, 'Who are you?'

Friar could feel Clara's dread bubbling to the forefront of her mind. He could hear her synapses firing as her thoughts began to ricochet around in her head, telling her in a very high-pitched voice that there was an intruder in her home and urging her to grab a weapon, scream, phone the police and to run back inside her room and lock the door, all at the same time. He only had one shot at this. If he failed to calm her down, then her drunken brain would spiral into hysteria and she would be beyond his control. He couldn't afford to let that happen. Friar took a step towards Clara. He dropped his hood and gave her his widest grin.

'Clara,' he whispered reassuringly. 'Don't worry babes, it's only me.' Clara's mind was slowing down now, confused. She said, 'Friar?' Clara rubbed her eyes. 'Friar, you scared me. What are you doing here?'

Friar sighed, it was working. 'I think I left my phone here. I didn't even notice until I was nearly home and, well I ain't going home to get shouted at for losing my phone again,' he chuckled. 'You know how jarring my dad can be when he gets going.' Friar began to conjure up memories in Clara's head of a tall, stern father figure.

'But how did you get in?'

'You gave me a spare key, remember?' Friar told her, and Clara found that she did remember. 'You told me that if I was locked out or anything, then I could just chill at yours.' She was convinced. All he had to do now was send her back to bed and get out of there. 'I didn't think you'd mind if I—'

There was a heavy whine of brakes as a van pulled up outside. Friar could hear footsteps walking up the path, alarmed mutterings from outside. *Fuck*, he thought. He was so busy dealing with Clara that he'd let time get away from him.

'Fucking kid's been here,' growled a voice. It had a thick Irish accent.

Clara looked dangerously like she was about to cry out, but Friar was already behind her, both hands covering her face. He could hear the sound of boots walking over broken glass.

'He's done a real number on this place, Tuesday,' one of the robbers called in a stage whisper. The Irish voice, that Friar guessed was Tuesday's, let out another curse. 'Little shit. Go check upstairs, there might be something up there that we could sell.'

Shit. Clara was panicking; he could feel it dripping from her, seeping into him and clogging the inside of his head. He needed to leave. If they caught him here, they'd skin him. *Focus*. He needed to focus. Clara's bedroom door was still open. If he could get to it, it might buy him some time to escape. He moved backwards, dragging the struggling Clara with him, until he was inside. Using his foot, he pushed the door to and stood there, listening to the heavy footsteps grow louder as they ascended the stairs. Clara continued to squirm in his grasp like an enraged cat. Twice she almost let out a squeal and Friar had to tighten his grip over her mouth so that her heavy breathing hissed against his hand. Now she was kicking out and digging into his arms with her nails. Friar gritted his teeth, as a hot wave of anger swept over him. What a stupid bitch. It was already her fault that he'd got caught up like this – if she'd just stayed asleep, he would have been gone ages ago. And now she was making his life even harder by wriggling around and clawing at his hands. He dug his fingernails into her face and felt her flinch in pain.

'Shut up,' he hissed in her ear. 'Shut the fuck up.' He wrenched her head sideways, squeezing hard. Outside, Tuesday's man was shuffling through the debris of the other rooms, commenting on how much of a mess Friar had made. He sounded almost impressed.

Clara seemed to have got the message and had stopped struggling. Friar exhaled. 'This wasn't how it was supposed to go,' he whispered, 'but if you do what I tell you, we'll both get to live through this. Got it?' No response. Friar gave her a shake. 'Clara,' he said. 'Got it?' Realisation struck him, that he was carrying her full weight in his arms. His eyes widened as he noticed that her hard, frenzied breathing had stopped completely. No! Friar sat Clara against a wall. Her eyes were partially closed, but Friar could see, even in the darkness, that the pupils had fixed. Fuck, no. Friar was sweating now; his eyes were watering and there was a metallic taste in his mouth. He lightly slapped

Clara's face and her head lolled to one side. Panic rising, Friar remembered how frightened Clara had been, how she had struggled and clawed at his arms and hands. His hands that had been clasped tightly against her mouth and nose so that she couldn't make a sound. Friar's world melted. In the darkness of that glass bedroom, only one thought coursed through his mind: he was going to go to prison. The police would find evidence that he'd been here, they'd link him to this. He'd killed someone and even if, by some miracle, it turned out that Clara was still alive, he'd get life. It was over. A noise outside the room brought him back to the present – a rustle and a clunky thud in quick succession, which sounded to Friar like someone tripping over a large bin bag full of stolen goods. He could not believe that the night had gone this badly.

A cry of 'What the fuck?' told him that it was definitely time to leave. He turned frantically towards the window. Like the rest of the house, it doubled as one of the bedroom walls. Friar hefted a desk chair in both hands and hurled it at the window. As the door was flung open behind him, he launched himself out into the night.

'He's in here!' shouted a voice, but Friar had already clambered out of an immaculate hedge that lined the perimeter of the house, and was vaulting over the fence and away.

He ran for a long time, his ears ringing, his stomach doing backflips. He needed two things. The first was to be sick, which he did in a bin in Crouch End. The second was food, which he found in a rundown Dixy Chicken shop not far away from where he'd thrown up.

The server looked at the wild-eyed youth who came blundering into the restaurant. Not many people liked to eat here, hell, *he* didn't like to eat here, but he was certainly used to kids in hoodies turning up at all hours, especially on weekends. The haunted look in this kid's eyes, however, made him uneasy; no doubt the police would be following him in any minute now.

'You alright, lad?' the server asked.

'Just hungry,' the kid mumbled, looking back towards the door expectantly. The man nodded. Definitely in trouble with the law.

'Can I… um…' Friar gulped. He needed to calm down, but the events of the night kept playing in his mind and every time they did, they showed him a new detail that he had missed the first time – her pink, polished toes as her feet kicked like a new swimmer, the spray of spittle as she struggled for breath beneath his hands. 'Can I have six hot wings? And chips.'

The man raised an eyebrow. 'I'll make that to go, shall I?' he asked.

'No. Eat in.'

'Oh, well if you're sure.' The man hollered Friar's order behind him to the only person in the kitchen. Then he said, 'Have a seat.' Two minutes later, Friar was sitting by the window, nursing his chicken and watching the sun rise, and wondering sadly if it would look the same from behind bars. He was sure that by now, his employers would have found Clara's body. Would they go to the police? No, he thought, that would put them in the frame for the robbery. Friar's eyes widened. No, they wouldn't call the cops, but they would be present at the scene. The bastards had been all over that place before they had clocked him and, from what he could hear, they hadn't been too cautious about where they put their feet, or about how much noise they made. He let out a manic little laugh, which attracted a strange look from the server. It was so simple. All he had to do was implicate them in Clara's murder. It was pretty much their fault that she had died anyway, after all he wouldn't have had to go back if they'd just agreed to pay him. This would be retribution.

He thought back to the last time he'd been in this deep – things had quickly spiralled out of control and he'd considered running away. But he'd managed to pull through in the end. And he would do the same now. All he needed to do was to keep calm and use his head. But if he was going to succeed, he'd need help.

Chapter 5

'Dead?' Rhu stared at Friar in disbelief. The more she tried to wrap her head around what Friar had just told her, the more her mind railed against the thought. She hadn't known Clara, except in passing, but that didn't make the thought of a dead classmate any easier to comprehend. He nodded grimly.

'I got there ready to rob the place and there she was.'

'Oh my god.'

'That's not even the worst part.' Friar scratched his head. 'The worst part is that now I'm involved. I gave whoever killed Clara the way into her house. That puts me in the frame.'

'How is that even slightly worse? And why come to me with it?' Rhu got up and began pacing slowly around her room, running her hands through her dark hair.

'Well, I'm not going to go to the feds am I? Imagine how that would go down. "Excuse me officer, but I found this dead girl in a house that I broke into." And if the police find her body with evidence of me being there, they're gonna get the wrong idea.' Friar looked sidelong at Rhu. 'But if we got there ahead of the police, did some digging of our own…' He gazed at her, a smile playing on his lips.

She stared back at him incredulously. 'What? What the hell does that mean? "Do some digging of our own?" You mean hide the evidence?'

Friar made a flippant gesture. 'I guess you can put an ugly

spin on anything when you use negative terms like that.'

Rhu took the TV remote from where it lay on her bed and moved to throw it at Friar's head.

'Hey, don't do that!' he exclaimed. 'Why are you so violent?'

'Fuck off!' Rhu snapped. 'Just piss off, Friar.' She stood before him, the remote still raised. Friar made a conciliatory gesture.

'What have I said that's so wrong, Rhu?' he asked. 'Do you think I want to get put away on false charges?'

Rhu turned away. 'We are not going to mess with evidence.'

'I didn't say we were.'

'Oh, I'm sorry,' she retorted, 'I forgot you have your own little names for your crimes. What do you call this one then? Housekeeping?'

'Look, it's not even that deep. All we're going to do is go over there and get rid of all the bits and pieces that would confuse the case by drawing me in.'

Rhu gave him a withering look. 'Oh, so we're doing the police a favour, are we?'

Friar cracked a smile and she turned away. 'No,' she said firmly, 'I'm not going to get dragged into one of your "adventures" again, especially not after the last time.'

Friar looked genuinely confused. 'What did I do last time?'

'That boy in Broadwater Farm.'

'What about him?'

'You told me that we were going to pick him up and drive him to Edmonton.'

'And we did.'

Rhu gritted her teeth. 'Where he was jumped by six guys with metal bats.'

Friar scoffed. 'Well that's neither here nor there, is it? Wait, you mean you locked me off over some petty shit like that?'

'What?'

'Okay,' Friar said, holding up his hands. 'I'm sorry that I misled you. But Rhu, this is different. I'm not lying this time, I promise.'

Rhu looked at Friar, at his pleading expression. She felt herself waver slightly.

'How about this,' Friar said. 'You help me with this and I'll never ask you to come out with me again. Just don't leave me to take the fall for this, Rhu. Please.'

She sighed. He was a lying, manipulative bastard. But he was no killer.

'Fucking fine,' she said. 'What do you need from me?'

Friar smiled. 'Well, for a start,' he said, 'I'll need some new shoes.'

SHAKIRA IRFAN

Letting Go

I began to walk on the side of the road
with the view of the window where we hugged last.
The glare of the sun on the glass erased the shadow of two
broken people,
and a love that was too afraid to grow.
I learned to substitute coffee for tea
while I thought about the twenty different sessions, just to
understand.
I was looking through a paper hue
out into a world where I was a villain,
pacing around a city that went on as normal while
I asked myself why.
A hundred coloured emails a month slowly became single digits
and I'm waiting now.
Waiting for the love in my heart
to seal my preconceived rules for living shut.
Waiting to walk away.

Grandmother

She liked to remind me that, even when it was hard,
hope would only ever be buried under the layers
of hurt
by me.
But she said in her language of course,
with her soft, ageing voice that was raspy when she whispered.
The pleats of her sari would cover her hands,
where her wisdom was sealed shut in the grooves.
One day,
a man from the neighbourhood stood in the doorway of our home,
speaking of a woman's role, a man's name and honour.
I saw the end point of a smile on her face,
but I didn't understand.
I knew she would tell me later, in her soft,
ageing voice.
My hands in hers,
she would tell me later.
In her language of course.

Breathe

And one day, I will sit down with a mug of coffee.
Maybe not in the house of my dreams.
Maybe not with the love of my life.
I will hold the warm porcelain between my palms and look
  ahead, look around.
I might see nature around me.
I might see other people tapping away at laptops or
having meetings that mean nothing to me.
I might be looking around
at my version of a living room.
I may not be exactly where I want to be in life.
Wherever I am,
whatever I am looking at,
one day I will sit down with a mug of coffee
and say,
'For now, this is enough.'

A Blue Sky

Each morning I feel like a paper boat.
And if the wave that deconstructs my sails
Comes today, I only have one wish.
To be lying inside the warm patchwork quilt
On this bed opposite the wall with our family portrait,

To be sheltered by the scent of our books
And the sight of the jade plant you water too much.
And don't forget to play the piano piece I'm
Too tired to remember the name of. Most of all,
Let me hear your voice painting the life we shared.

I can hear you now, but the sound fades too quickly
These days. But I know you, and you are pacing up
And down the corridor, shouting into the phone and
You only ever shout to help me. In my mind, I'm taking
The phone out of your hand and promising you that

I have everything I need in your fierce selflessness.
I have become the heaviest plank of wood, splintering
The hands and shoulders of those who call me Dad,
Uncle, Grandpa and I hear you say 'my husband' down the phone.
And to you all I say, thank you and sorry – a thousand times over.

I turn my head and look out to a blue, blue sky,
And I can see the sun shining.
I wonder if it is the same as yesterday's sun,
Or if it will last as long as Thursday's sun.
It is easier than wondering if
It will be the last one.

SOPHIE CRABTREE

Bobble Hat Blues

She fumbles about in her wibbly wobbly wellies
splattered with a mud, grass, leaf cement.

Only one marzipan-yellow mitten remains,
which she gums off and spits on the carpet.

She lunges for the cat who spots her bright
red overalls marshmallowing towards him.

He squawks when he's not quick enough
to escape the duvet-padded strangulation

that passes for affection in her saliva slick palms.
A kitsch-clash printed double bobble hat

cushions her but falls off as she wrestles him
to the ground. Tired girl. Dad locks eyes

with the cat in apology,
who blinks, finds a purr.

Forgetting My Sandy Ice Cream

I drop my gipping goat grimace
as a peel of laughter spins me round
in my wonky deckchair.

It's coming from the blonde todd running ahead
of the pram they've loosened themselves from,
straight into the frothy shallows.

Their squeal sucks up into my glum guts
as said pram is planted on the sand
and they are plucked from their paddle

and dunked in the deep:
chunky little legs like churros in sugar.
Again! Again!

Incense City

That scent is cause to run off from that house and clutch the merchant through a sweaty, sweary summer of scrapes and smiles. It's cypress that stains your soul long after it washes from your skin.

Cash-strapped and dazed by all the dauntless things you dared do with it in your lungs – tearing up Incense City, getting wilder, darker – you only stay in that house and take the kicks under the table until you've saved enough, made enough playlists to see you past county lines.

Another scent inhaled. This one stickies-up your insides, makes them heavy with the confusing notes of bergamot and bleach that you've got to remind to be nice to the waitresses. You leave this one in a hotel bathroom for the reassuring emptiness of a split-lipped leather diner booth a few towns over.

You're too worried about scraping pennies together for hot chocolate to remember that you should feel guilty for not being in that house another bad Christmas when the scent of summer whips you around on your stool.

The very perfume bottle you had grasped in your fist like a bike throttle stands before you. 'Fancy seeing you again,' your half-whisper, three tan shades and a heavy heart lighter.

You catch its cedarwood fingers, loop them with your own, and drag them out onto the pepper-cracked tarmac once more.

Resentment

Resentment left this morning.
He picked his shoes up from next to mine
and fastened them sat on the front step
with a face full of sunrise.

Suicide Bay

No matter the time of year, half-empty bodies follow their noses to the malty damp air that clings to where the world splits in half.

The sea cries out as the next braces herself on calcified railings. Her heavy heart drops to her boots as she escapes the cliff's jaws and stomps down on its gritty tongue.

It gargles up a salty spit to awaken and avert her. The caw as she scrunches her face echoes the screeching seagulls circling the sky; it bats around the empty seats of the amphitheatre.

The wind tries hitting her back into one of the seats to catch her breath, only to leave her wanting more of the lime pang chasing down tequila. The thunder curses.

Show me! she says.

She is saturated, shivering, undeterred. Drunk on driftwood.

She orders, Another!

Tsunami sand burns her cheeks.

Another, another, another. Cry after cry she takes the assault with the same resolve as a member of a pirate's crew staggering about their brig, goading the sea.

The sea shakes its head, pulls her into its arms.

VINCENT OTTERBECK

I Could Care Less

I should be taking steps
But I can't really see
I should hold my head up high
But your thoughts weigh heavy on me
Focus more on the journey
But I can't find my way
I would speak up for myself more
If I knew what to say

Sometimes I feel like running
But I can't run from my point of view
Always somewhere else in my head
I promise it's me, not you
Focus less on myself
But I'm scared I won't be enough
But I really care lots about you
And that at least is the truth.

Skating with Halle and Torin

Sky twilight blue
The three of us
Cruise down the road
Orange streetlight glow
Black hoodies and bleach-blonde highlights
In the tunnel
Layers of spray paint litter the pavements
Broken from the walls
Cars drive by, towards the dead end
Once they pass through we get back to it.

Thinking

Sunrise
Sunsets
Days go by that I forget
Sure enough I've got regrets
But I just move and go and get.

Sister

Same city
Different streets.
I was happy to get cupcakes from her friend's house when I
  went to collect her
But I never thought why I had to go.
Same strangers
But they're not a threat to me.
No one breaks my boundaries
And plays around with me
As if I were an object and not a person.
Same house
Same parents
Different talks.
No one put the fear in me
Because it was not necessary.
Same keys
But I never conceptualised mine as a weapon.
Same clothes shops
But was I ever made to feel at blame for my choices?
No.
I get a passing glance.
They get the male gaze.
Different bodies
Different outcomes.
I didn't realise that roaming freely was a privilege
Because I never paid attention.

Mum

What's one word for something that holds this life together?

Another Day

What lie will I tell myself this time
to get through it?

Gift

You shine so bright!
I love to watch it
Your smile is the best gift
Your thoughts light me up
You are something special to me!

Make Me What You Want

Take me
Twist my form
Make me
All the things
You want me to be
Turn me
Into something good
For you
Break me
And put together the pieces
Just right
I'm waiting
I just want to be
What you like
If I knew
What you liked to see
I would paint myself
That way
Tell me
How to be
I'll be that way
Change me
If that's what you need
If that's
What it takes
Teach me
How to get it right
For you
If it were possible

I would do it
Be new
Be something good
For me
By being good
For you
Make me
What you want
Please tell me
That you can

On People I Love

To my friends
you're like glitter
you colour my world

To that one person
you're like the sun
you light up my space
but if I tried to look directly at you
my eyes would burn

To Feminine Boys

I think you're beautiful.

Cold

Shiver.
My hands go purple when I'm outside, but
my mind is blue already, anyway
things don't really add up to me
and I have bad eyesight anyway.
What's one thing you can't live without? Pressure.
And I push myself every day.
Dreaming is my holidays, time
for me to get away, live
to see another day, okay
I don't care anyway.

I just write,
I don't know if it's true to my life.

A Story

Once upon a time there was a being, who said
'Help me. I don't know how to get by in this world.'
And the answer smiled, and said
'Everything you need is already inside you.'

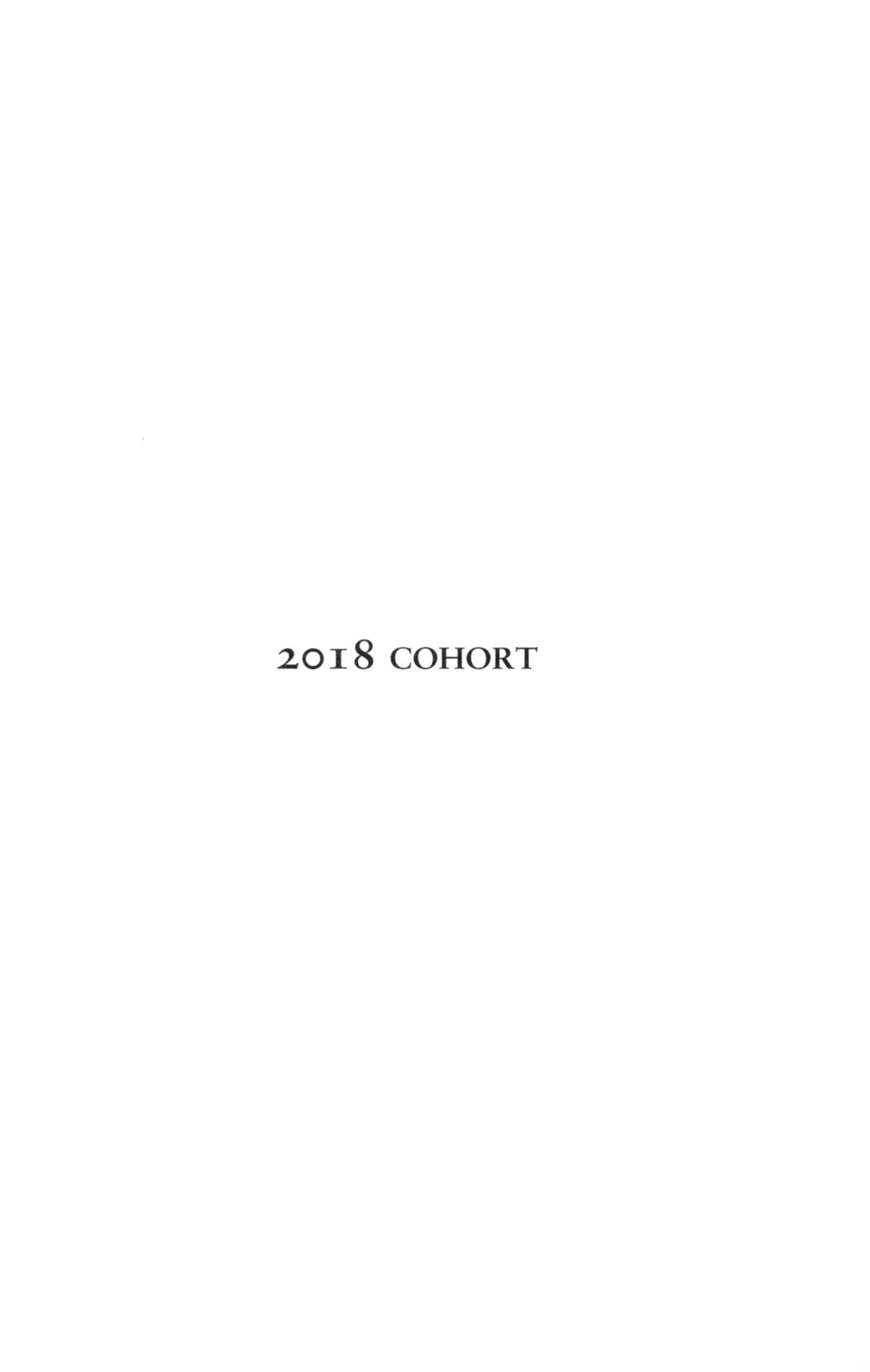

2018 COHORT

AISHA BORJA

Mother's Day

She glares, she growls
from across the room,
feet up on the sofa,
reading the blurb of a book
on Mother's Day.
She's two arguments in today
and she's on a roll,
sulking evenings.
My sister's in the kitchen
with incense, making
a friend's recipe with
her headphones on high.
She can't hear me or herself but
can watch reflections dance
in the windows that become
mirrors after dark.
I'm sitting between them,
equal length away from both. Now Mali's sieving flour into
a bowl in a rhythm,
by her feet the baby of the house,
our cat, waits.
Like this house she is pregnant,
literally looking like she's swallowed
a water balloon. I think we can all agree
motherhood doesn't fit something that's
barely a year old.
My great-grandma birthed
her first child at thirteen. Her
childhood soaked into

the thing she cradled and
the wedding photos that
look like me dressing up
as a princess in preschool.
These quick comparisons
make me sick of plastic babies
and Haribo wedding rings,
where teen pregnancy
and Year Six puberty lessons
are the beads my great-great-grandma
counts on her rosary.
Jesus y mi abuela Teresa.
Jesus and my grandma Teresa
who's probably sitting in a rocking chair
in the most populated house I know
surrounded by great aunts,
content.
I look up at my own mum.
My sister puts a tray
in the oven and shuts it with her hip.
These evenings, let me be grateful
for the beings who care
for the fragile so I am able
to grow and make my own mistakes
and choices.
I raise a toast
to my mother who has just started
re-reading *Love in the Time of Cholera*,
light over her shoulder imprinting
a shadow on the wall behind her
like a halo.

This City Forms Intimacy That Knows No Privacy

I'm watching two bodyguards
Dancing ballroom in each other's arms,
Half listening to unenthusiastic
Street magician's audience applause.
London's benches,
Uncomfortable, like art,
Like concrete blocks.
Coming here never feels unwelcoming
But no one ever stays or sits
Still, movement is international
And restrictive.
Waiting, I become invisible,
Fading like graffitti at a skatepark,
Not like a Banksy,
Never that prestigious,
But always that political.
A demo voice in this city,
Like everyone else,
Trying to make it.
London's like that, loud.
Eight million people telling a different story
Under the same roof
Though not on the same floor.
We all try and touch the stage
For a second, then when it's done
We all stare, but then move on,
Stand back for a minute,
Watch the tube fly past,
Forgetting that artist's name,

But remembering their struggle,
One of the many
Lionesses of London, not sorry
For being there or
Being smart or
Knowing their shit unlike the dicks up there,
Parliament standing,
The architectural embodiment of a hangover.

Fat

This is not the brain I wanted
so I'm changing it, cutting the flesh
around my head, sifting through hair
until I hit rock skull, bringing out
a hammer I'll knock the end of the knife
gently at first, listening for a crack,
getting impatient I'll start hitting a little harder
and when I hear a crunch I'll stop
and open up to see grey pink yolk
in a yellow bone bowl.

I'll pull her out
and place her on the weighing scales,
watch the fatty worms slump a little,
see that as expected she is overweight,
then I'll move her to the chopping board
and start cutting, slimming her down
until she's hot girl summer ready,
then I'll scoop what's left and
put her back in. Sew a few loose veins
together, let my eyes roll back
and wipe the blood from my forehead,
hope for the best. As I walk I'm sure
I'll hear her rock around
in a skull three times too big.

Bring Me a Baby

and make it labelless, no genitalia or race,
no skin, just a pile of jellybean organs,

bring it here
and let it crumble in my arms
while I sing it labelless songs as it lies
wealthless

and by that
I don't mean without wealth but
unaware of the concept of wealth,
coins just metal portraits of a woman's aging,

let the baby be born
from no one and let it only understand
noise without language.

Now let's put it in museums,
let's take it to court and parliament, let's
let them put handcuffs on its bloody wrists

and then free it again,
make a statue of its detached body,
then when the world gets too uncomfortable

skin it,
and by that I mean the opposite

put skin onto it,
gender it, give it two parents,
christen it and feed it, let it see
colour and language and wealth and

as it grows
slowly tell it about
the world it grows in,

tell it about death
and slavery and war,
tell it about the fashion industry,
overproduction, abortion, diagnosis,
time,

the police, illness, trafficking, traffic,
what's right and
what's wrong,

make it understand
make it sad
make it helpless
make it want to help and force it

to keep growing.

Darkness

in the flat before we arrived, early and large.
We brought more in the £6 wine, extra in Jack's

leather jacket hung over my shoulders, drowning me.
Darkness in the kitchen speaking French with the models

too tall for the low Peckham ceilings, necks at a 90-degree angle
as their words slipped out like murder, darkness

watching gay and inquisitive straight bodies in the bathroom,
in fact darkness came in to turn off the light. Darkness

in the echoes of the guitar and the boy who played it.
Darkness turned down the music and asked me

if I had a boyfriend, his monobrow and pretty uniqueness
from afar suddenly too close. Darkness in the shuffling

dance steps in the living room. Darkness hugging
the edge of the balcony while we smoked and listened

to the process of being threatened in London the way
the man (because it will be a man) shows you

the knife he will kill you with, tells the time frame
in which he wishes to do it as smoke and darkness

rise and whisper. Darkness in the host's bedroom,
and I think that's when me and Jack left. Darkness

at the bus stop and the songs we sang on the bus.
And there must have been darkness in the pizza

we curled over because there was darkness
in my stomach the next morning.

HENNA RAVJIBHAI

Ba

You shuffle in faded plum slippers
loose silk sari leaving behind
a glittering snail's trail of memories
which dance between knitted brows

eyes mist behind Your tainted
gold-rimmed spectacles, sitting as
You pick at the dried chapatti flour
under turmeric-stained fingernails

smiling vacantly, mouth open
forming shapes instead of words
I ask if You know my name You
just keep smiling, placing a

garland of white carnations
over Your head as the fire rises

Ward 12b

'Are you wanting to join me or somethin'?' he chuckled.

I hadn't realised I was heading for the wall. I turned around to see him sitting upright, matching the grin of his Noddy toy doll which as always is perched up next to him at the head of the bed. He looked the same, wearing an odd pair of pyjamas, 'because even though it says you can wear 'em together, don't mean you have to'. Eleven years old and had already cracked the system. Also, he just wanted to be Captain America and Buzz Lightyear at the same time. He radiated the brightness of the room in just one smile. Instantly, I was at ease. I went over to hug him, careful not to step on any wires that would get me in trouble. Dad warned me before we arrived not to touch anything otherwise we'd have to pay for it. We weren't in any place to pay for damages nor was I to argue, so I fidgeted with my bracelet instead.

Mum was hiding in the darkest corner of the room, mute as a swan though barely as elegant; she had aged almost a decade. Blotches of mascara had dried up under her puffy eyes, which she couldn't be bothered to wipe off. Her lips would wobble into a smile and crack at the corners. When we hugged it felt like she was clinging onto a lifejacket.

Sensing that the attention had diverted from himself, my brother began to rattle off the itinerary of procedures and operations with big words that I couldn't understand. The nurses came over and laughed, claiming that he was going to steal their jobs. Apparently, he had already complained to the chef that the standard of food was lacking, and that he wanted something tastier if he was going to be eating here for a fortnight. I'll admit I was slightly jealous at the prospect of having jelly and ice cream every day, but he was having none of it.

My brother continued to chew everyone's ear off, taking full liberties in the limelight, but the glow never seemed to rub off on my mum, who had taken to rearranging the Marvel comics we had brought along with us into alphabetical order. Dad and I had spent nearly an hour deciding which ones to take, but it didn't matter in the end. He barely glanced at the comics, believing that after all these operations he was going to become a superhero. I guess he would be, to me anyway.

* * *

We're here again. I've memorised the walk to his ward, though something is off. Maybe it's the dried milk stain from my uniform that we didn't have time to change before we came. I carry a giant 'Get Well Soon' card that everyone in his school class made and signed for him. Loose bits of glitter fall behind me as if I were Hansel and Gretel leaving behind breadcrumbs. Dad wanted to carry it, he said that I would ruin it, but I refused. When we arrive at his bedside, nobody is there.

A nurse comes up to tell us that there was a problem with the operation and it is taking longer than expected. He should have been out two hours ago. Dad asks where Mum is, the nurse whispers in his ear so that I can't hear him, but his legs buckle with whatever news she gives him. I'm left on my own waiting, hoping that I can see my brother soon so that he can tell me off for not smiling or eating all his chocolate digestives. I leaf through some of his comics, wondering what special powers he might acquire. I hope there isn't any gamma radiation around – the last thing I want is a giant green brother.

The nurse takes me to the 'Creative Corner' where kids from other families or recovering kids who have had their operations can come and play. I find a dot-to-dot book, which has over a hundred dots to join, and start on that. Some kids come and join me and I don't notice them at first, but it's Harry and Jack from school. Their cousin is in hospital too. They distract me for a while, we make jokes and pretend that we're auditioning for *The X Factor* using water bottles as microphones and wearing tin foil like wigs.

I was just about to butcher 'Breaking Free' from *High School Musical* when a bed wheeled past. The silence was more audible than our singing and the occupant on the bed was thin, pale, his hair was swept messily across his face and tubes were sticking out of his mouth. It was only when Mum and Dad followed behind holding hands as they talked to the nice nurse with monkey ears that I realised it was him.

The surrounding colours drained, mixing and muddling into the same muddy green walls as I tried to recognise my brother's face. For once he wasn't smiling. Noddy was clutched to his chest and he didn't want to see anyone. I wanted to cry but I didn't know why.

I guess I was expecting a superhero to emerge with a ferocious energy and special abilities, looking immaculate, about to save the world. The glint in his eyes never dulled, even though he was only a crumpled child in pain, holding onto his toy and wishing to go home.

She Only Came for the Food

She likes this part of the hall.
Here she can *clip-clop* across wooden flooring
in two-sizes-too-big plastic pink heels,
trying not to trip over her bejewelled pistachio green
and rose-pink suit whilst sticking back on the bindi
that has fallen off for the third time.

Within the rows of impossible folding tables and chairs
and that white paper lining which rips without touching,
she marks her spot. Carefully draping her shawl across
two chairs, saving one for her big sister who
failed to escape the grasp of fussing 'Aunties',
squeezing your cheeks, saying how much you've
grown even though they only saw you yesterday.

Swinging her little legs from the chair, she awaits
the arrival of giant steel pans swimming in saffron syrup
and hot *masala*. Finally emerging like a scene
from *Beauty and the Beast*, guests accompany
the parade, plastic compartment plates in hand.
Greedily she asks for three puris and the largest gulab jamun
from the tall one-gloved men standing behind the pots.

Before devouring the sweet stuff first, she waits
for her sister, who comes back with more *bhaat* than *dhaal*.
They sit together in matching suits, bargaining over
prasad and counting the amount of sakar and
those sugar-coated almonds like gold bars,
reluctantly exchanging her Maltesers for a Bounty.

The hall is alive with a kaleidoscopic
chatter, scraping of chairs and loose sequins,
smiling brown faces singing, all drumming
to a familiar rhythm to which she danced
the whole night in her plastic-pink *clip-clops*.

2019 COHORT

MARIA CLARK

Seat H6

Every Tuesday, at twenty-five minutes past two, Ricardo sits down in seat H6, Screen 2. It's in the back row, centre-aligned, and almost directly below the projector. The whirring and crackling might have disturbed another, but after almost twenty years, it's as natural to Ricardo as an orchestra warming up their instruments.

The projectionist arrives at quarter-to, feet clattering on the metal catwalk above. When the council proposed to convert the old boot factory into a cinema, there was uproar, but the plan moved swiftly onward, cutting and dividing the factory into smaller rooms, like one scene folding into another. The catwalks crisscrossing the factory ceiling remain, projectors and speakers balancing precariously.

Ricardo can still remember the day the cinema opened. The scent of boot polish is faded now, but on that first day – when the enormous doors slid up and a few lamps blinked the way to the screens – it was as pungent and as fresh as if the employees were still working there. The film – he can't quite remember what – was some sort of Western, but all he could think about were the rows of labourers, mending and fixing and scrubbing the manufactured boots with polish.

When the projectionist arrives, Ricardo takes off his coat. The seats are leather, capturing the heat of the previous occupants, but he still has difficulty thinking of them as anything but the original flimsy tartan. Bus-like.

The film starts at three. His *hijos* always complain about the tardiness of modern cinemas, and the wave of adverts determined to wash viewers out of their seats, but the old boot factory has always been the same. Two adverts, two trailers, and then the film begins.

The seats beside him are rarely occupied. The back row is perched on the edge of a precipice, like the tips of the mountains visible from Santiago. It takes a few minutes to reach the top, and though Ricardo has been visiting for years and knows the perfect way to hold his popcorn (tucked under the left arm: not too tight, not too gentle) and where to rest (Row D, lightly holding onto the banister on the right-hand stairs), most people don't dare. Those who have bought the back tickets look up, gulp, and then sit in vacant seats elsewhere. Part of it might have to do with Ricardo himself – an old paper bag, rustling and crunching his popcorn – but he's never had enough courage to ask.

The row is empty. He rests his popcorn on the left-hand seat, perfectly balanced. From his bag he extracts a bottle of water and a small pot. His arthritis winces against the screw lid, but soon the air fills with the sharpness of paprika and the salty tang of almonds.

The lights dim; he empties the pot over the popcorn. Sonja used to make it this way, stirring the almonds in on the heat, the corn jumping and flowering in the pan.

'Just enough to make it pop properly, eh, *mi corazón?*' she'd wink at him.

Row H doesn't smell quite as nice as their old kitchen, but the tang in the air settles his stomach. The first advert begins – a car advert, almost a film in itself – but his gaze is drawn to the harsh light spilling in from the open door. A silhouette slips in; then, darkness.

If Sonja were there, she would have been grumbling under her breath.

'*Idiotas… ¿Dónde está el respeto hoy?*'

He misses the sharpness of her tongue, slicing through the seats. It was as steady as the projector's beam, lasering through stupidity.

The curtains at the side of the screen twitch. Ricardo settles down in his seat. There was a time when he had ample girth to cover it – and possibly another, too – but now he almost needs padding.

It's a thriller.

Ricardo feeds upon the sweetness of anticipation. Part of the excitement is never knowing exactly what the film will be, or where he will be transported next.

A shadow falls across the seats.

He looks up at the silhouette, standing at the end of the row. There's no sound of breathing – despite the mountainous climb – and for a moment he is taken aback.

'Excuse me – is this Row H?'

The voice is young, girlish. Ricardo is distracted by the strength of her perfume – citrus, eucalyptus, blossom, like the trees lining the avenues back home. Before he can reply, there is a flash of a torch and a murmur of triumph.

The woman sinks into the seat next to him.

On the other side, his popcorn jumps, a few pieces tumbling to the black depths of the row in front. He grabs it and pops a piece into his mouth, reclaiming possession. The paprika explodes into his crevices, scorching his taste buds. When he starts coughing, the woman looks at him. Her face is sharp, elf-like. In the watery light of the cinema screen, it makes him think of the legend of La Pincoya, which Sonja used to recite to him at night.

'*Mi alma*, if La Pincoya came, would you be faithful to me?' she teased him. 'I'm not so sure, *tú sabes*. Blonde hair and beauty... difficult for a man to resist, no?'

The woman is indeed beautiful, but has to be the same age as his *nietos*. Ricardo smiles, getting his cough under control, and turns to the film.

It's difficult to concentrate. Her warmth, her scent – even

the way she rests one hand on top of the other – sends him scattering back through his memories. His *mama*, frying something on the stove, singing along to the radio. The taste of freedom and the smell of cedar trees, summer in Santiago, dancing on the bandstand under the indigo sky.

Ricardo forces himself to watch the film. A man, a flash of polished cufflinks. A malt whisky, side angle.

'My husband looks like that,' says the woman.

Ricardo looks at her. She hasn't taken her eyes off the screen, but is smiling softly, reaching out as if she can trace the actor's face.

'He's not that tall, of course. And he would never drink a single malt.'

She shifts, captivated. Ricardo hasn't seen someone so hypnotised by the screen since the place opened, and finds himself watching her, losing interest in the film entirely.

The actor enters a fight scene, punching and jabbing with the ease of a professional. Ricardo tries to find his voice, buried beneath the taste of nostalgia.

'But he doesn't act that like, no?'

The woman's eyes latch onto him: blue, burning.

'He's ever so brave, you know. But he wouldn't hurt a fly.' She pauses, biting her lip. 'Unless he really had to.'

The actor slips into a silver car, pressing a handkerchief against his bloodied jaw. Ricardo turns back to the woman, but she's gone.

* * *

The next week, it's a romance.

As a boy, Ricardo scorned them. He remembered playing with his father's cigars, lying in front of the television set, while mama and papá curled together on the sofa, lounging like cats in the sun.

Sonja loved them, of course. Her favourite: *Gone with the Wind*. She used to hold her hair up, looping it around like Scarlett O'Hara's, and bat her lashes, mimicking the slow drawl of the accent. Ricardo never understood her obsession, but after watching it every single year for her birthday, it gradually softened into a film he loved. Later, he would watch it over and over, and then glance at the sofa quickly, hoping to see a flash of Sonja's smile, or hear the muffled weeping she attempted to hide behind a cushion.

His attention is hanging by a very frayed thread – rather like those holding his buttons to his cardigan – and snaps when the silhouette appears. The woman says nothing, greeting him with a slow, careful smile, lit up by the yellow-and-pink ambiance of the film. She sits down.

The scene transitions to winter: the main couple, tiptoeing through the snow. The only time it snowed in Santiago, he was in school. He faintly remembers noses pressed against the glass; hurried exclamations from Señora Martinez. *Dios mio, hijos, mira!* It was as if the mountains had shrugged their shoulders in boredom, sending cascades of white spiralling into the city.

The shot zooms in on the couple, a snowflake landing on the actress's cheek. The actor tucks a strand of hair behind the actress's ear, a smile tickling his mouth. Next to Ricardo, the woman holds her breath. Her eyes start to overflow.

'Daniel does that all the time to me,' she confesses. 'And this scene… it's almost like going back in time. I've *been there*.'

There's a couple in the row in front of them; the man turns around, chewing on his hot dog, and glares. The woman next to Ricardo takes no notice.

'My husband's just like that,' she says, as the actors kiss.

'We're like that. Perfect for each other. It was meant to be, you know?'

Ricardo doesn't know what to say. 'You're very lucky.'

His words come out rusted with a bitterness he didn't expect, but she doesn't react.

'We're supposed to be together. No matter what.' Her voice drops to a whisper. 'I *know it.*'

The actors draw apart; the woman pats Ricardo's hand. Her skin is cool, but sharp.

He watches her walk down the stairs, limping slightly. As she opens the door, he sees a flash of colour on her cheek – purple? Green? – but her silhouette melts away before he can focus.

He puts his empty popcorn box on her seat.

* * *

She's late.

The slow, steady crescendo of the film soundtrack is gradually drawing him in, but Ricardo keeps his gaze fixed upon the emergency light above the door. She must be coming.

It's been so many weeks now that he has almost forgotten what it was like to have the back row to himself. The gentle whisper in his ear; the small, sudden fidgets in the seat next to him; the occasional laugh, or cry. Last week, he even let her try his popcorn. Her fingers were small, plucking out a solitary piece like a rare jewel from a treasure chest, and her eyes nearly swallowed the entire room. She promised that she'd bring him something in return, and now he sits and waits.

It's nearly halfway through the film when she appears. Her silhouette is fuzzier than normal; her ascent, slow and hesitant. When she reaches Row H, she takes a long breath, and uses her hands to manoeuvre herself to her seat.

'Daniel had an important meeting today,' she says, quietly. 'I couldn't leave – not while he's working from home.'

The way she lowers herself into her seat – hands gripping the soft leather; a wince escaping her lips – transforms her from La Pincoya to an *abuelita vieja*. With a headscarf, Ricardo thinks, she'd look rather like Sonja did in those last few days.

Ricardo offers her popcorn.

'How are you?'

She hesitates, wiggling her fingers, but then shakes her head.

'I'm... I'm here,' she says. 'That's all that matters.'

It's a horror. Twenty years of bloodsucking vampires and haunted houses and this new cyber-supernatural *chorradas* has left Ricardo unfazed, but he still grimaces at the sound of the screams. Next to him, the woman is silent. She hasn't even removed her coat.

The scene changes to a husband and wife. She's on the floor, bloody; he's wielding a belt. Ricardo can nearly smell the tang of blood and swallows, looking away. He sees the woman next to him gripping her chair, so tries to make a joke.

'Your husband isn't like that, is he?'

The woman's eyes are flecked with fear. She blinks twice, and then looks down at her feet.

'No.' Her voice is fragile, a tightrope stretched between the peaks of the Andes. 'Of course not.'

A moment passes.

'No,' she says again. 'He can't be.'

Conviction is punched into every syllable, but there's also something else. The hint of a question.

She's still there at the end of the film. The same position, the same expression. As the lights turn on, Ricardo notices the large winter coat covering her body, and the bruise on her cheek.

'*Mija*,' he says. 'It's over.'

'I know.'

He struggles to his feet, but she hasn't moved. 'Do you need a lift home?'

For the first time, she looks at him. Her eyes shatter into pieces, crumbling before him.

'It's over,' she says. 'Isn't it?'

'Yes.'

The woman shrinks in her chair. 'Are you sure?'

Ricardo takes her hand and helps her to her feet.

'That's up to you, *mija*.'

She swallows. 'My husband...'

She's holding onto Ricardo's hand so tightly that it nearly snaps.

'I'll take you home,' Ricardo says.

That Tuesday afternoon, he leaves seat H6, holding the woman's hand and walking her down the stairs. She doesn't say a word. As he helps her into his car – her limbs trembling like those of a child – he thinks of Sonja, making popcorn.

His heart, cracking and bursting, would fit in the pan perfectly.

MARIAMAH DAVEY

The Plan

This was the last chance. The only chance. To save, not only humanity, but Mother Earth herself.

Ian took off running at the sight of them. The Lackeys, or whatever they called themselves. He knew it was only a matter of time. They were everywhere. Uncivilised, half-witted slaves, who would do anything for the protection of their rich handlers.

Unfortunately, for the rest of the people on this godforsaken planet, it meant that they were well-equipped for their mission at hand. Which was to find the very thing Ian was protecting. He was pretty certain the Lackeys didn't know of him, only the existence of the plan. Which was already a problem.

Ian dived behind a large rock. They were close, and a moving target was as enticing to them as an injured animal was to a starving human. Easy prey. Not that there were many animals, mostly insects. Luckily, they drove straight past in their modified buggies. He had seen, one too many times, people getting torn apart by their vehicles.

Ian watched as they drove off, hunting for more prey for themselves and their masters. And hunting – not only for animals. He pushed the horrifying thought aside and stood up. He needed to get to Svatsum. The one place he knew where his best friend and fellow scientist was hiding out. The only place he knew where he could work on the plan and hopefully save the planet.

As Ian stood up his world spun. Trying to keep steady on rocks was not easy, but he had a lot of experience with this particular situation. For the last few years, the air had become thicker, he felt as though he could take a bite out of it some days. After the dizziness faded, he began walking once again.

Unfortunately for Ian, the Lackeys weren't the only people he needed to be cautious about. Desperate times call for desperate measures, as the saying goes. He didn't blame the people trying to survive by any means necessary but the Lackeys were at an all-time low.

Ian was hoping he would be able to find a government post. Although usually far apart and ransacked by Lackeys, they did give out free fresh water and food. If he was lucky, there would be filter masks, but usually the rich and powerful had already bought them all for themselves and their Lackeys.

Ian pushed forward, tightening the straps on his bag and readjusting his sunglasses. He made his way onto flatter land. Although doing this increased his chances of being spotted, it also increased his chances of finding a post. That was the thing about survival, it was a balance. A balance between risk and reward. Choices had to be made with half the knowledge necessary to make the decision. It was a matter of life and death and, in Ian's case, the life and death of humanity and the planet itself.

When he felt a drop of water slide down his cheek he prayed. Although rain may seem like a survivor's best friend, it was more like a friend who you never really knew whether they were going to stab you in the back or give you the world's best hug. It was that unpredictable. Either way, when the rain picked up Ian stopped. He reached into his bag for his two empty water bottles and sat down on the ground.

Even the rain was warm. He took this moment to survey his surroundings, although quiet and bleak. Ian took note that he was in a valley. He felt the wind and rain beating his face as he turned towards the mountain to his left. The rain began thundering down and, although his bottles weren't full, Ian threw them into his bag and began running as fast as he could. At that moment, he realised he had made the wrong choice – now it was no longer in his hands whether life or death took him.

The valley began filling with water, and quickly. It was only a matter of time before Ian was swimming, getting thrashed around by the speeding waters. Every time the water was generous enough to let him peek at the air, Ian took a breath only to be thrust back in seconds later. His body began to grow weak as he tried to fight the water. He was a strong swimmer no doubt, but this was a force no human could fight. Ian felt helpless as yet another wave knocked against his chest, winding him. As he tried to catch some air he was dragged under, taking in a breath of water. In his last conscious moment, he reached up desperate for life.

Ian awoke on his side, a pool of liquid beside his mouth, which he imagined was his own. His first thought was the USB. He clasped his chest, feeling around. It wasn't there. With the little amount of energy he had left, Ian sat up and looked around, only seeing three shaded figures. He watched as they turned around and came closer to him.

'Oh, he's awake.' The older man spoke, glancing at the woman, who nodded.

'I didn't think he was going to make it at first,' she responded.

Ian didn't know if these people were survivors or Lackeys but, then again, he had never seen a Lackey group with a child before.

'Um, I had a pendant, it was around my neck…' Before he could finish the woman threw the pendant with the USB attached at him.

'Here you go, I didn't think it was best to have things around your neck while you were choking on water.'

Trying not to give away the importance of the pendant, Ian offered a grateful smile.

'Well, thank you. Have you got my pack as well? I had better be off.'

Ian stood up and put his arm out.

'Nonsense, you nearly died not too long ago. Let us get you a meal at the very least. Survivors take care of survivors.' Her smile was bright, along with her blue eyes. Although her clothes were dirty and her hair slowly matted, her personality radiated.

Ian knew that it was hardly the case that they took care of each other but they did rescue him from almost certain death. The least he could do was keep some manners and humanity going in such difficult times.

As they all sat in the small room, Ian noticed the little girl. She seemed happy playing with her rocks but had a terrible dry cough.

'What's your name then?' the woman questioned handing him some cooked cockroaches on a stick.

'Ian. What are your names?' Ian asked, trying to make conversation. Cockroach wasn't his favourite, but food was food.

'I'm Ellen,' the woman pointed to herself. 'This is Dag.' She pointed to the older man who tore into his meat like it was his first meal in a week. Which it may well have been. 'And this is Cho.' Cho looked at Ian with glazed eyes, brushing her short hair off her face.

'Where are you all from?' Ian asked as he watched the woman scoop up Cho and place her in her lap, encouraging her to eat.

'We're from here – Norway – but the little one was born in Korea and came over here when she was a tadge,' Dag answered as Ellen nodded along. He lowered his tone to barely a whisper. 'Her mother passed near the beginning on the desolation.'

This was one of the many, many reasons why he needed to get that plan to Svatsum. He knew the sound of that cough. He had heard it too many times, lost too many people to the pollution and bad air.

Ian asked, while fiddling with his pendant, 'Do you guys have anywhere you want to go in mind? Any family or friends?'

Both shrugged, diverting their eyes. Ian's lips tightened. He knew he shouldn't have asked that question. Too many people had lost family and friends to this. It was a given...

'I was wondering if you'd like to join me?' Ian wanted to continue and say that they would be assisting in saving the planet and all that lives on it but, alas, he couldn't. He trusted them, mostly anyway, but he knew no one could know of the plan and its whereabouts.

Dag ran his fingers through his coarse, grey beard. 'Why? Do you have a place in mind?' He stared at Ian.

Swallowing, Ian answered, 'Yeah, in fact, I'm on my way to Svatsum, I have a friend there.'

Dag's lips twisted as he looked at Ellen whose blue eyes glazed over. She offered a single nod.

Dag turned back to Ian. 'How far is Svatsum then, friend?' Dag lifted his tattooed arms up.

Ian felt a smile creep onto his face. 'A few days' trek, but it's worth it.'

Dag didn't return his smile and his jaw tightened. 'Your friend.' Ian watched him as he stood up and sheathed a blade in his belt. 'He's no rich bastard, is he?'

Although Dag didn't know Ian or his friend, it was almost as if he felt the cold of the blade pressing against his throat, making him sit up. 'No, of course not!'

Dag opened his arms wide in celebration. 'Then we'd be happy to join and meet your friend.'

Although Ivan, Ian's friend, was no 'rich bastard', he did have a house and security, but mostly for protection against Lackeys.

Also, in order to keep safe and in hiding, waiting for the day when Ian would arrive. Once was enough.

'I'm sure he'll be happy to meet you guys.' This time they all shared a friendly smile.

Dag wrapped a protective arm around Ellen who readjusted her blonde hair. 'You get some sleep guys, I'll keep watch for tonight.' Ellen looked as though she was about to argue, but Dag cut her off. 'Get some rest, I'll be fine.'

Although Ian never liked to part with his USB, he rarely slept with it on because he often ended up sleeping on his stomach and the risk of breaking it was too much. He took it off and placed it in his pack and drifted off to sleep.

As he awoke, he noticed everyone else was still asleep except Dag, who sat carving a piece of wood with the knife he retrieved earlier. 'Morning sunshine! You can go back to sleep if you want, you've got a few hours until daylight.'

Ian sat up and walked over to sit by Dag. 'I'm alright thanks. Why don't you get some sleep, I'll keep watch,' Ian offered.

'Maybe… maybe after I finish this.' Dag chipped wood pieces off the block.

'What is it?'

'A doll for Cho, she always plays with rocks, it's not good for a kid. I remember having dolls.'

Ian nodded knowingly. 'Where were you when everything messed up?' he asked.

'Well, I'm not that old, man! I'm only sixty-four!' Dag laughed, slapping Ian on the back.

Ian laughed along.

'True. I meant to say where were you when society collapsed and realised we couldn't go back from this'.

Dag nodded. 'I was at home with my wife. Our house was raided by Lackeys. She was murdered.' Dag took a deep breath, running his fingers through his beard, almost tugging on it.

Ian stumbled on his words. 'I'm so sorry, I shouldn't have asked.'

Dag gave a weak smile. 'It is what is it, unfortunately, you can't do anything and neither could I.'

But that was the problem. Ian could've done something. He knew he had tried but he could've done more. That's what he was doing now. Correcting his foolish young mistakes.

'What did you do before this?' Dag questioned, trying to make conversation.

Ian tried to hide his sudden fear, playing with the hem of his top. 'Lawyer. You?'

'Engineering,' Dag answered, looking at Ian a minute with questioning eyes but deciding not to question it further.

Ian turned around when he heard shuffling.

'Hey, Cho! You okay? What are you looking for?' Cho looked up and saw Ian. She gave a cheeky smile and ran off back to her mat.

Dag rolled his eyes. 'See why I am making this doll now?'

Ian's smile widened in response. 'Very true. Bless her. A anyway, I'm awake now Dag, you get at least a few hours' sleep.'

Dag's lips tightened and as he was about to argue, Ian ushered him over to his sleeping area.

'I'll keep watch, stop worrying for once.'

Dag got as comfy as he could, given the fact that he was lying on the floor with a thin mat.

'But that's the only thing that's kept me alive for so long.'

Ian stood outside and watched the sun rise, creeping up from behind the rocks and mountains. The orange glow was something familiar and warming. His heart felt lighter in that moment of peace but, alas, it was called a moment for a reason.

The earth began to shake. Ian watched as the rocks on the

ground bounced around. At first, it seemed as though it was a small earthquake, but he quickly realised what it really was when he heard shouting getting closer.

The Lackeys.

As they were in a building, regardless of how small, they were a prime target for the Lackeys as they were hunting for equipment, food and water. So was he and the other survivors. The main difference was that the Lackeys hoarded. They took so much more than they could ever need, regardless of other people.

Ian ran inside. He didn't want to shout and scream, he didn't know how close the Lackeys were. He knew only one thing. He wanted to avoid them.

He crept towards Dag and pushed him lightly. Dag jumped up, staring at Ian.

'What's wrong?' Dag's look tore Ian's soul apart. He knew facing the Lackeys once again would pain Dag. He hoped it wouldn't come to that.

'The Lackeys... they're close.'

'Faen!' Dag exclaimed. He rushed and woke up Ellen as Ian woke Cho.

They could hear the Lackeys getting closer and closer each minute as they packed their goods.

Ian was sure to put his USB back around his neck. As much as he had started to care for the others, the USB was priority.

That was the moment when the Lackeys burst through the door. Dressed in their usual masks, long-sleeved tops and skinny jeans. Equipped, of course, with any and every weapon they could get hold of. Bats, balls, hammers, logs, rocks were common. Less common were swords and guns but they still got them on occasion – from their masters, of course.

'What is it we have here?' the first guy asked, swinging his bat almost as if practicing.

The moment they grabbed Ellen by the arm and began smiling maliciously, Dag charged at the leader but to no avail when the leader swung his bat and knocked Dag out cold. Ian watched helplessly as the blood pooled on the floor. The leader whistled and the next minute a cloth bag was placed over Ian's head and he was dragged away. He didn't even know if the others were brought along.

The light blinded Ian as he struggled to open his eyes. As they adjusted to the light, he saw Ellen, Dag and Cho tied up beside him. He saw tables, chairs, computers. Something felt… familiar. He tried to reach towards them to comfort them. To whisper everything's going to be okay… but he didn't know that.

'Hello, my old friend.' The voice spoke in a deep tone.

Ian's heart dropped when he recognised the voice. That voice, this room. It all made sense all of a sudden. It was his old 'friend'.

'Pfff! You've got an interesting concept of friend there...' Ian scowled back.

Dag called out to Ian, 'This is your friend! I thought you said he wasn't a rich bastard.'

'He wasn't when I left… What happened?'

The man's forehead wrinkled even more than before. He stroked his greying eyebrows. 'Do you want to know?'

Ian nodded. His last memory of Ivan was of the beginning. When the Lackeys first discovered the plan and raided the lab. Ivan gave Ian the plan and let him escape. That selfless person. Now, this.

'It's simple really. After you escaped, I struck a deal. If I could control some Lackeys and not get killed, I'd help them get the plan off you. And here you are.'

Ivan let off a small giggle, proud of himself for keeping his end of the deal.

'So, I know you've got it.'

Ian tried to shuffle to comfort himself, the plan swinging around his neck.

Ivan came even closer and grasped the USB in his hand. 'Ah, so ironic, you always did like pendants.'

Ian shouted out in a desperate attempt to stop this horror, the only chance to save the world in the hands of a mad man. 'We will find a way to save the planet and end the reign of you monsters!'

Ivan gave Ian a sympathetic smile, almost as if he was a child. 'I remember when I was naïve like you but hope without justification is pure idiocy.

As those words bounced around Ian's mind, he watched as Ivan released the USB, letting it drop to the ground. With a muddied boot, he slammed his foot down, cracking the plastic case. With another stamp, the plan and the planet in one fell swoop. Gone.

Ivan smiled to himself and nodded to the Lackeys who stood watching. They made their way over to him and his friends.

'So, first you end the world, now you're going to end us?' Ian scoffed.

'If only it was that simple. No.' Ivan licked his lips. 'I'm setting you and your merry crew free; you can go along your way. The Lackeys won't bother you anymore but you'll live every day with the knowledge that the world will end. You along with it, of course, and there is no hope of fixing it, not this time.'

Ian almost wished they would just shoot him, end it. He wished he'd have known how much of a psychopath Ivan really was… all those years back.

The Lackeys untied Dag, Ellen and Cho along with Ian. Their heads hung low as they walked out. Ivan called back one last time.

'Oh, Ian! A present.' Ivan threw him a USB that looked

identical to the first. He remembered buying them together when they got the lab.

'Memories, I suppose.' His sinister smile scarred Ian's mind as he clutched the USB in his hand and left.

He had almost forgotten about the blazing heat for a minute when they exited the lab.

'So, do you want to explain a thing or two?' Dag asked. He didn't want to snap at Ian but he was furious.

'Long story short. I worked with Ivan as a climate scientist for many years. When everything happened, we had already been working on a plan to reverse climate change if it was to get too bad. Which it did.' Ian took a breath, trying to be mad, both at himself and Ivan.

'We got raided by the Lackeys and he let me escape with the plan.' Ian played with the blank USB he had in his hands and felt a sharp pain in his finger for a moment. He looked down and, although no blood, there was a small scratch. He looked over the USB and, as if the universe had granted his only wish, the back of the USB had 'The Plan' scratched into it.

He remembered scratching that himself the first time he decided to download the plan onto the USB. Ivan must've got confused and given him the wrong USB at the time. Ian had been carrying the blank. Now there was hope with justification. Ian smiled, looking up.

'Want to help me save the planet?!'

NIDAA RAOOF

Lost in the Waves of Wisdom

I am lost.
Lost between the waves of wonder.
Lost between the waves of wishes.
No map. No compass.
No mind can draw me back to freedom.
But I am drowning.
Drowning in the confusion. Your wandering words went
whispering among the absence of my love for you.

Underneath the water's echoes, I fall soundlessly.
For I am still searching the ocean. Searching the sands of time.
I am surviving the waves' wrath alone.
The waves' force exerts its darkness upon us.
I need a light to extinguish the darkness.
But I cannot find it – the light. So I will forever keep looking,
until I do.

Your meaningless words will float adrift. Move astray.
Fall between the parallel mirrors of the earth's clockwork.
Buried in the sun's dying embers my shadow rose.
The hand it gave pulled me to my feet to gasp for air, to gasp
for that breath of freedom.
The beauty of the confusion is the patience in that moment.
The strength of the sea will never devour the aeonian
resilience of my soul.
Go ahead.
Come for me with all your power – if you dare.
Written in the water lies the truth.
Painted on the waves' glass surface, a reflection of the stars
silently shines.

Hidden in the power of the darkness the light guided me. I could not find the light.
So I decided to become it.

Amber

Gentle sunlit rays embraced the blissful peach sea of warmth. Sapphire clouds of darkness lingered above the thunder-struck waves, beaming with lightning.

The melting sky kissed what was left of the land goodbye, leaving peculiarity as foreign dust among its shadows. Every soul became lost in the Earth's nightmares and the trees, one by one, stopped casting their cool shade on the ground. Every atom was lifeless. The planet was ready to die again tonight, but the people were not – only this time the sun would be gone forever.

Spring's Love

A hundred things standing in front of me.
Yet a million things have been pushed behind me.
A cool breeze.
An amber glow whistling alongside the wind, through the trees
 and into my window.
Sun resting on the floor, shining over the cats.
Rainbows hiding in every corner of home.
The year is new. So is my mind.

Happiness

Warm glowing sunshine bleeds into the sky's clouds.
Gentle rays of comfort fall onto every raindrop.

New air fills my lungs.
A cold mist sits in mid-air.
The temperature bites your fingertips.

A rush of heat rises upon your face.
The day is fresh. The night is at rest.

Where Sky Meets Sea

With every radiant sunrise,
Your violent waves crash with rage.
Your temperature cuts the skin from blood.
You stare silently,
Your voice roars in agony.
You rest your body at the horizon.
Only when the sun begins to bleed do you stop killing.

A Mother

As perfect as the last blossom in the middle of summer.
With petals as pretty as the tree's ancestors.

Like the comfort found in the voice that sits with you in the dark.
With a sound as sweet as a robin's first chirp.

As precious as the first snowflake falling in winter.
With beauty as distracting as a sunset's colours, as they bleed
through the clouds.

Like warm rays of light resting on a cold shadow.
With love as everlasting as the sky's existence.

The last blossom. The voice. The first snowflake. The sun.
Not a single word, metaphor, poem or book can describe a mum.

Artist

Creativity falls from your fingertips with a rhythm like no other.
Oh, look at the way the paint bleeds from your brush.
Cartridge skies flourish in your mind.
Each graphite line, curl, circle and swirl almost like words.
And every piece of art you create with a message of its own.
Oh, if only more knew how to read it.

The Enchanted Grove

The summer sun sat in the candy-blue sky, its warmth made a peach nest around itself and the clouds. The birds whispered to the leaves, which rustled at the touch of her feet. She felt every breath of fog and every tickle from the howling wind. Whenever she visited, she felt as though she was in an enchanted forest. A forest with the ability to hold her happiness and remind her to sm:)e when she felt down.

A broken tyre-swing hanging from the trees. A hobbit's door at the bottom of an oak tree. Helicopter leaves hidden in the glimmering grass. This was home.

Glowing eyes. Burning warmth of the sun resting on her face.

Hair down. An inspiring breeze brushing through it.

She was home.

Alice Lost Her Way to Wonderland

The amber leaves settled where the sun tickled the horizon. The whispering winds brushed the branches' elbows. Autumn knew Alice wasn't far from magic. There was frost freezing her nose and a breeze blowing under her dress.

Alice ran. She ran as far as she could. Quickly and quietly. Autumn's presence wasn't far, and neither was its power. From the rage she carried in every step, Alice skid across the glistening leaves.

A force like no other held her down. But this wasn't Mother Nature's act. It squeezed her ankle tighter than the rope around her heart and pulled her down. Only this time it wasn't the White Rabbit. It drew her into a vertical tunnel of mist. Blood lined the walls of her throat and the mist had stolen the warmth from her lungs.

Alice had reached the ground. Only this time it was to meet her death. Death screamed her name with anger. Never again could she visit Wonderland. Never again could she see the only family who loved her. She had lost her Wonderland.

A Sanctuary of Hope

Running. Running was all she could do to be herself. It was the only way she could hide. Inside the city's crowd of screams, shouting and stress she became lost. So she reminded herself of what she could do. Run or stop?

Her heart pounded faster and faster as she bolted from the world like lightning. With the mindset of nowhere to go or hide, she was losing all hope. Running past cars, heavy roads and swaying branches. Running past the pressure. Running away from her worries. She soon found hope. Hidden between the loud buildings and busy roads she stumbled.

Stumbled across a sanctuary. A sanctuary of hope. She had never seen a place of beauty like this before, yet it was here all along. Stonebridge – her new place of hope. A home with animals and kind people. A home which showed her where true happiness lay. Another family. Another forever home.

Say Their Names

A world where racism is a pandemic.
A world where one name can ignite a flame of fear and anger in hearts.
Arrogance not allowing us to heal. Words cutting like a knife.
A world where staying silent and patient has become powerless. Voices are our only weapon. Protests and gunshots fighting over who is louder.
Has the planet not crumbled into more than enough pieces already?

Victims' names scream in our heads a thousand times.
Dismissed by those of arrogance and privilege.
Those who tap, scroll and slide past each sign. They swipe through all the stories and posts – and they slowly become blindfolded with ignorance.
Each name. Every clue. Unable to comprehend the pain from their blindness.

Their heavy words and violence have snatched away comfort.
They forget we all bleed the same colour.
They ignore history.
They haven't let you breathe.
They refuse to remove the blindfold.

Please. Stop. Take a knee. Pause. And find your stolen comfort again.
I beg you not to draw that knife. I beg you to keep fighting with your voice.
We know it has been too long. We know there are too many names.

You are not the colour of your skin. Or what you dream to win.
You are not the clothes you wear. Or how you tie your hair.
You are not the way you talk. Or the way you walk.
You are not the scars on your skin. But you are the battles you have won.

You are the diamonds that have appeared from the infinite pressure.
You are the sm:)es on your faces. And the voices that roar louder than lions.
You are the people we couldn't live without.
You are the ones who will change us today and every day after.

You are the history books. You are the power of love.
You are the ones who started building but got torn down again and again.
You grew into flowers but got pulled out of the ground.
You have been like stars in the daylight.

But you built your walls high around yourselves.
You sprouted from the ground again.
You found your way into the night sky – and there you shone.
But the the sun hasn't set for the last time yet.
If this nightmare continues, I will sit with you in the dark until the sun shows its glowing love again.
I will hold your hand and never let go.
I will not let you fall again.
I will make sure you can breathe.

The darkness will come again and again. But while we wait for the sun, allow your stars to shine as bright as ever.

And although the world may never change, we'll stand tall and strong.
And find peace and comfort in each other's voices, love and company.
We will use this power of our comfort to conquer this pandemic.

White Flag

When you almost stop breathing.
The ground shakes as you start running.
You fall.
You fall as though nothing will catch you.
Empty, overwhelmed.

You clench your fists to stop the shaking.
You stare at the sky and pretend that you aren't breaking.
They cannot read your mind, so you pretend there's nothing to read at all.

You fight for lost ambition, but the world has nothing left to save.
You swim to stop the drowning, but don't see the anchors on your feet.
You search through lost and found, for something that never even left you.

You listen for the whispers of reality hidden in your nightmares.
You explore the stars for Mars, but refuse to leave Earth.
You wait for a superhero from a different universe.

So, you blink twice to hold back the tears.
Spinning and spinning. And your tears blur your world.
Screams echo inside your head.

You pursue the sun at night.
You fly softly, but remember your wings are broken.
You run swiftly, but your legs only crawl.

You refuse failure, but your body stumbles again.
You jump from mountains, but there is no ground beneath you.
You run to the ends of the earth, but forget the world is round.

You call for help but the world is mute.
You cry snow but the world is blind.
You scream fear but the world is deaf.

So, you close your eyes tight, unclench your fists one last time,
and you rest your body on the shaking ground.
Your every nerve is trembling.
Blood runs around your body, searching in its pain, like a maze
– until the blood is no longer yours.
Your body fights again.
But your mind has fought its last round.

So, once more you blink to hold back those tears, but you've
already poured an ocean.
Once more you press your palms against the floor, but the
ground simply keeps shaking.
You're just too broken to raise your white flag.

WERONIKA BARONOWSKA

On the Line

The air is new and cold and scary.
White cliffs make my head spin.
This is it, my feet hit the land and I know this is it or I have
nothing.
There is a shoulder, a hand or a leg.
Keep my belongings close, hold on and don't let go.
Is my passport here? I check again.
Follow the stream of people, this is new land after all.
Immigrants on top of each other.
Maybe I'll get in.
They ask questions, I barely understand them.
We are locked in, I see cameras beeping red in the corner and
I sit.
I check my pockets, passport's still here.
Small windows and four thick walls. Take a deep breath.
My wife is waiting. My kids need clothes.
I hear whispers of farm work, wonder where I will live.
It has been three days, they ask questions.
Clutch that bag, sleep on the bench. There's no space.
Ask the questions.

That time I got locked in a graveyard pushes me into December snow

he is a contrast to the white
so dark it cannot be black
you walk past him quite often
but you don't want to notice him
i see him locked away
his name is thick on your tongue
but he knows more people you could ever hope to
he helps the old
picks up the young
he pets each dog that walks past him
he is my friend
i meet him after a crash
there is white like the snow that's falling right now
he only raises his eyebrow and i laugh
i have known him for years and this time
with a roll of those eyes i hit the cold
he is amused i can tell
so my own eyes don't open again

i do wonder what awaits me under the Christmas tree

Play a Game

Alexis was holding in her breath. Both of her hands tightly clamped over her mouth, desperate to calm down her heavy breathing. Her bare shoulders were digging into the tree behind her, the tank-top being the only material covering any skin. The shiver that ran down her spine only made her aware of the coolness that the night had brought in. The noise of heavy footsteps was advancing towards her, a constant heavy thump on the hard ground. A steady rhythm set on the stage that was the forest floor. A straight path, that she hoped wasn't set on her. Her eyes scanned the surroundings, taking in as much as the darkness offered, before seeing her salvation. A single light shining through the cracks between the trees. Something so far, and yet seemingly reachable. She remembered his words, the purpose for this entire act was right in front of her. The light was a sign of her victory.

'All you have to do is reach the road on the other side of this forest, then I'll let you go.' The playfulness that accompanied those words was disturbing, but it only boosted her motivation to move. To think her actions through.

The steps stopped in their search, and Alexis dared to take a peek from behind her barrier. Right there was the broad back of her attacker, his head unmoving but she could tell he was waiting. With a silent but confident breath, she reached for a branch laying at her feet. With no material rubbing together to give her away, she let the object fly through the air. The landing was almost booming in the stillness of the forest, and she couldn't help but look at the older man. Legs flexing in readiness to run.

She was met with emptiness, the grand mass of muscle was gone from where she left him, only minutes before. The unknown location of the man had brought the dread back. She turned back towards the light and continued with her plans. Legs started to straighten out as her whole body changed direction. Her eyes caught the glimmer of the light that was beckoning her to hurry up. One step, then the second and soon she was sprinting once again. The closer she got to the light, the more she realised how this didn't feel right. The light was right there, but there was no sign of a road, not even a trail that could have been made. The single light was sitting in front of a cabin, a small wooden shack standing alone. The windows broken and wilderness crawling up its abandoned walls. The exhaustion was now catching up with her. With slumped shoulders, Alexis fell to the ground. Her bloodied knees taking the force of her whole weight. She could only wait for the shadow to fall upon her, the porch light being completely hidden from her view.

Wild

The snow is heavy around his boots and he takes a moment to take a break. With a couple of deep breaths Mark sets off again, the distant shouting ahead of him is enough of a distraction to ignore the cold seeping in through his clothes. His friends aren't too far away but the sound of falling snow disorientates Mark. His mind is racing and he grips his backpack straps harder. Looking up, he sees the back of Alexander, almost unbothered by the extreme weather he is dragging them through. Looking behind, Mark notices Igor standing still. His back also facing Mark as he looks out. Mark can only assume he is looking out for any cars coming through – they were off the main road, but out in the open it wouldn't be too difficult to notice them. They didn't have much time to get changed back at the farm so they trudged through with black clothes, a huge contrast against the white now that it was day. He was lucky enough to score some gloves before they left the city. Mark cringes, thinking back to the clothes he brought with him originally. The suitcase was probably gone by now, God knows where his belongings ended up.

The group walks for another two hours before Mark notices a few houses to the left. With a shout he points towards them. Alexander just waves his hand and changes direction, leading the three to the buildings. These were different to the ones from last night, not a farm but not too far off either. Several buildings forming a square, a few bikes sat near what looked like the main house. They head towards it, this time Igor knocks on the door. A young man opens the door. Mark looks at his face and can tell he wasn't expecting anyone in this area. His voice is deep and accent thick. It mixes with Igor's slightly higher voice and Mark zones out. He looks towards the property. He doesn't understand a single word the men are saying and only looks back when Alexander calls out to him.

'They let us stay the night, but in the other building,' Alex says. Personally, Mark prefers his voice over Igor's, it sounds friendlier. Mark takes a long look at his friend. Alex does not look so good compared with when he first met him the other week. After years of talking online, Mark was excited to finally meet Alex. He owed him a lot. Alex had been a friend when nobody else had but Mark was not ready to forgive him for the situation they were in now. Igor was Alexander's childhood friend and partner in crime. Alex mentioned that they do everything together, so it didn't come as a surprise to Mark that Igor would be the cause of this mess.

'Did you tell them why we are here?'

'No.'

That meant the end of that conversation and Mark's anger begins to flow thicker through his body with every minute. He curses under his breath but keeps the complaints to himself – they'd all had this conversation several times. Now that Mark had finally sat down, he lets his body relax and his brain work through the stress. This room looked very similar to the one at the farm – the family had been nice and let them stay in their actual house. They offered them warm milk and even shared their food even though there wasn't much of it. They told stories and their youngest son even knew some English. It felt nice to laugh and meet new people.

Mark's hands begin to shake the longer he sits still. Last night everything had gone well 'till around four in the morning. Everyone had been asleep for a few hours by then and when Igor woke the small group up, with a finger to his lips, he pointed outside. Mark finally realised he heard cars pulling up. Alexander had come to the same conclusion and began packing. They were moving with haste and, without making much noise, they were out of the house in no time. They had barely been walking for a few minutes before screams echoed in the open. Gun shots followed quickly and then there was silence. Mark tried to look back, but Alexander's strong hand on the back of his neck stopped him. His friend didn't say a word but Mark understood.

The grim thoughts didn't leave. He prays this time will be different.

Love is Such a Strange Thing

I'll find a nice boy soon Alice says
I wonder about Lucifer the show is good and I don't really know if it is accurate
I'll have to look in the Bible I found a nice 'me' already
people talk about butterflies and magic
I feel magic in the first bite of my McChicken Sandwich
Can you imagine being a devil
must suck to sit there with the dead for centuries
would spilling sauce onto my white shirt count as a rejection
Love is a strange thing
Lucifer finally finds love too
I do prefer realism though
doubt Satan is that good looking

makes you do stupid things my mum said

my stupid is listening to all of them

Lucifer rebelled against his dad

I'll rebel against mine and God too

... Both me and Satan brought a nice girl home

Summer Feels...

I watched in curiosity as the girl kept twirling, her bare feet on the grass and brown curls lifting as she spun, arms spread out as she smiled into the sky. Bright yellow skirt flowing with the movement. I felt the same heat of the sun on my skin as she did, a sense of joy washed over me.

There was something about her that screamed freedom, all I can do is watch and absorb the feeling. I cross my arms and lean back on the bench, taking in the scene. Families walk past me, children running around the park. Joyful screams in the distance mix with quieter chatter of passing people. The grass seems greener than usual, or maybe it's just me. I can smell the freshly cut grass. I laugh at a sneeze behind me, summer allergies making themselves known.

I look back at the woman across from me, now standing still. The smile not once has left her face.

When was the last time I let go like that? My own hair feels too tight, pulled into a slick bun. My watch tells me I only have ten more minutes before my break ends, cold coffee sitting beside me, forgotten. I take in one more deep breath, soaking in as much of the sun as I can before standing up. With one more glance across the park, I stop at the sight. The girl is looking at me, and when our eyes meet she gives me the biggest smile I have ever seen. Pink dusting her cheeks. I look behind me just in case. Nobody's there. She sends me a shy wave and I can't help but smile back.

My own cheeks feel red. Maybe I have some allergies too.

2020 COHORT

ALICE IMPEY

The Truth

is turquoise,
a sea of stolen biscuits
and reeds of accusation.
The truth is puppy-dog eyes
and squeezy hugs,
the 'I don't mind'
when you're itching inside.
The truth is the moon.
When the tsunami smacks its lips
with a chef's kiss.
The truth, a glance.
The dog ate it, I promise.

Poem

Tastes of spiralling
Dripping
Senses
Let me find him
Speak his name
Swaying the empty roads
To be held
To be free
Talk to me
Stay
Breathe

KATIE PARKINSON

Milk on the Floor

on his way home from the office,
in a car of mortifying age and make,
mulling with a furrowed brow
over another bad day,

he hits a cat,
limp and black on the skid marks
and the tarmac, superstition
or a self-fulfilling prophecy,

and the sight of all the skewed,
blood-milk bones makes him a monster
for a moment, for the children
of the neighbourhood.

he shuts down, rubs the
back of a debt-folded head,
and prostrates himself for
whoever might come,

for his normal apology
and two ordinary hands,
at the wheel of an inferiority complex,

leased by the wages
of a middle-class man,
who hit a cat
on his way home from the office

Roadkill Comfort Food

what is it i'm looking for
when i see death

staring blankly at the road
on an open evening, watching
the paint slipping under our wheels,

as the wind whips up some
white flagging pigeon, clean feathers
ruffled in the highway rush,

and it's fresher than what i've grown used to,
an impression of mincemeat spilling into the floor;

i once joked that a rabbit had
burst into raspberries,
when i felt it was getting too much,

a quaking thing who was
looking to be lulled back to sleep
by an innocent, empty old road

Chronic

it's during the kinder times of
a seasonal affective disorder
that a mutiny makes up my skin.

it comes in lumps and growths,
desert-like, and i come for it with an army;

on nocturnal mornings, i wake up
with four claw mark-smattered limbs,

and confuse scars for canvas skin,
or the marbling of a hot-blooded creature.

in a way i am inevitably captivated by it,
how my flesh, unwillingly, will harden and break;

how i unthinkingly ease it
through self-mutilation;

how it feels like a metaphor,
and probably isn't

Bath Water

i tilt my head one day
and hold the bath water in my ear,
to hear the rumbling, like a war drum,
instead of my thoughts;

when i was twelve i caught myself
bleeding in ireland, doubled over in
a public bathroom and watching
myself in the mirror, doing the same

under a showerhead much later that night,
frightened and fascinated by the bright,
tensile pearls, coming away and
floating around my still swelling thighs;

with my head stuffed between two invisible hands,
i can sometimes sit still enough to
maintain the surface, watch the grime and hair
in my toes from the day sit quietly
on top of the ripples,

and imagine my mother died violently
in may, then make myself cry till
my whole face is red, take an hour
to cool down my weak, salt-burned skin,
in the great, ugly well of the bath water

Milo

i've fed him again, watched his
tiny, trembling jaw hike down a weekly
meal with anxious attentiveness,

turned the lights off, and tucked
his stacks of bagged baby mice back
into the pit of the freezer, think about

how the impulse to love him
has numbed me to their fresh smell,
fragile in death, and remember what
every website maintained

as i researched how to
recognise infections in reptiles;
it may tolerate you,

its tolerance cannot be love.

and i think of last week, how
he sat around my shoulders,
face buried in my hair,

how i felt his tongue, like a
dandelion seed, on the rim of my ear,
his blatant lack of fear,

and i wonder if i were
transcribed and researched,
like an animal bred for
humane social consumption,

would they take care to note
how this fire-head child,
avoiding its mother's gaze,
felt safe in her company.

i look at his body, muscular and bright,
half-buried in substrate that sets off my allergies,

and know that we will never be shown
that kind of mercy

A Singer in Memphis

where are you when your voice
is bleeding out of my ears,
and i kill another album for the trophy shelf;

when i think of you as magic, long-fingered
and supple-tongued, like something holy
to be worshipped with fake grace
on stilled knees, the soothing of
an eardrum-buried speaker,

or when i think of you as heartbreak.
it never takes me by surprise; i just brush
up my own fragility and pay you no mind,

i'm thrown by shapes and noises,
but we follow them like god, to the
violent end of the fabric
way we know each other,

when you sing another beaten-down
cover of a drinking song,
and i write another poem about a car

PRIYA GILL

Farm Bills / Hard Pills

The farmers in India left their lands in peace,
but you're deliberately waging a war whilst tearing up roads
and now you have them begging on their hands and knees –
sadistically staged it; you don't even care enough for hope.

You are deliberately waging a war whilst tearing up the roads.
How do you expect these people to put food on the table?
Sadistically staged it; won't even care enough for hope.
Shooting inexplicable abhorrence, they're abused and disabled

and you expect these people to put food on the table?
This outright discomfort is shameless hurting in public
through inexplicable abhorrence, they're abused and disabled
for feeding the country; the most valuable service for nothing.

This outright discomfort is shameless hurting in public
and now you have them begging on their hands and knees
for feeding the country; the most valuable service for nothing.
These farmers had left their lands in peace.

Minestrone Soup

Are we really gonna have another passive conversation
about the way he looks, and then hits his homie?
Don't eye me like that, as if you haven't got the patience.

As if there's no good reason for these 'random connotations'.
All the poor girl did was forget the minestrone,
and we're about to let this become another passive conversation?

Don't tell me it's a savage observation!
The way he treats her, it's a whole different zone, see
you know it too. Please don't tell me you haven't got the patience.

What happened there, it's different to a marriage obligation.
She's so closed in, deep down even sinners know she
really doesn't want this to become another passive conversation.

Look! I'm not saying we can fully plan an operation,
but I don't expect ignorance, just 'coz you didn't know he
was like that. Don't lie again about your apparent loss of
    patience.

Bro, this is the reason she's part of the damaged population.
The safe life isn't just for you – winners only.
This really is becoming just a passive conversation.
How can you say that you haven't got the patience?

Malala

Dubbed *the most prominent citizen* by her
Prime Minister, equality is what she came to serve.
For boys and girls to school together,
She just wanted to learn.

At age 14, shot in the head –
Stop with the mess!
She just wanted to learn
And allow girls' voices to be heard

Loud and clear, be proud my dear.
She just wanted to learn.
It was award-winning advocacy –
A Nobel Prize actually –

That gave her the space to learn.
A degree from Oxford,
An interview from Harvard.
Global accolade, awards for days,
The poor got paid.

The law engaged.

The Days When

Unlock the days of lunchtime football,
playing outside, where we had time
to slip, to fall, to rely on plasters.
Where you'd never catch us working in the library.
The way we stood in P.E. saying, 'please choose me!'
I want a time where we just lived for today.

Unlock the dreams before today.
I remember the biggest calamity being a burst football,
but you know the lads would always pay me
for it if they were guilty, though some took their time.
I want to mess about in the library
and only be worried about cracking the plaster.

Unlock the scent of sweet-smelling plasters,
how I wish I could smell them today!
I want to play Tank Trouble in the library.
Let me gather round a crowd and play desktop football
and impress you with my rhymes as you set me a time
in a life of trivia. That's all for me.

Unlock the joy of designing Nintendo Miis,
days when our wounds would heal with laughter like plasters.
I yearn for the taste of Mum's roast lamb with thyme.
Maybe I will try to recreate it today
whilst watching the 5 p.m. football
or listening to classics from my music library.

Unlock the taste of junk food feasts in the library
as we set goals of who we would be:
sell-out performers, professional footballers,
teachers, bricklayers, even plasterers.
I wonder where they are today,
and if they reminisce about childhood times.

Unlock a period of simpler times,
where it was tasking to navigate the vast local library –
how I wish to roam those halls today!
Each day brought a different life for me,
we'd slip, fall, rely on plasters
and look forward to the game – the joy of football.

I'm thankful today that life gave me time
to remember dreaming of football in the library.
I will wish again today for a nostalgic plaster.

Unsure

Before this, only dying meant remorse,
until one home-life got robbed; torn apart.
However tiny, scratches from divorce
sting forever, pain can stop a heart.

The army base, forgotten strength and life
deceased, a house unfolding for a child
provides a roof. Unpacking thoughts, a strife,
traumatic past... internal wars a' wild.

Depending on lines is how she survives,
reshaping backgrounds through her rhyme,
her lenses all night. They halt decaying lives.
Remorse, before this, only had the time

in life. Her mind designed a time whereby
her dying meant a life among the lies.

Spare Part at BMW

Today, *Phaji*, I wore that hat you brought me.
It kept me very warm, sheltered from the snow,
but did not do too well for my already haphazard hearing.

I'm getting to the story, don't worry! So...
I'm working on a convertible, on the assembly line.
Nigel comes up to me, a bit flustered, right,
says: 'S! John's car isn't moving?!'
Phaji, the smile on my face. I wish you were there!
Someone had asked me to help them. Me!

So I'm so excited I drop the wrench on my foot.
Hai, I might've said, had we not
invested in steel-toe boots six months earlier.
I leave the convertible,
and I'm practically Armin Hary
as I race out the door.

Jono was definitely there
and his car was definitely not moving!
The silly sod had left the handbrake on.
Can you believe it? The screech that came
from his car was quite magnificent,
in a bad way, of course.

So I say to him, 'Jono, take your handbrake off, init.'
You know how the *goreh* are when they get all embarrassed.
He was redder than his car within seconds.
'Thanks, erm, S,'
he mumbled, and sped off.

I'm sure he would have been more grateful
had someone else helped him.
Just like that, everyone was back to normal
and my 1.5 minutes of fame was over.
Can you believe it, *Phaji*?

SOUMYA SHRESTHA

I See a Painting of Vayu

A vivid image of a cottage life is carved in the ivory rock
inside a display case in this British museum,
yanking my consciousness
back to dwell in the comfort of my lineage, Nepal.

*

My ears recall a familiar morning crow as
the body of stone in front of me begins
to transform into thatched bamboo huts
and the rough surface of the carving grows
fainter under dense layers of fog.

*

In Duwakot, adjacent to the capital city of Kathmandu,
a rugged contrast of culture and westernisation.
The villagers' sluggish movements float
among the heavy smoke from burning logs
and the fog alongside the rice crops.

*

In this British museum
I see a painting of Vayu
sat on his gazelle vahana
darting his crow-like eyes among the people
unknown to his unforeseen wrath.

*

Oh! Lord Vayu!
Mercilessly riding on your shiny coach
with thousands of purple horses.

The air now heavy as your concrete and steel statue,
heavy as the rocks from the land deemed underdeveloped,
heavy as the people who chose to exclude
the richness of their culture and its essence.

*

Vayu, you release your cyclone towards this western air
I breathe, deriding me for neglecting my heritage
and the soil that supported me since my early steps.

*

Vayu Deva, defender of the north-west direction!
You chuckle away with your blasting
breeze and the neighs of your horses as I blink
away my tears under the limelight
of this British museum.

Memories of Godavari

The wet mud of Godavari beneath our shoes
as we dash across this slanted
rocky hill towards the glistening Bagmati River.

My friend Nima's laughter is a kind of company,
filling the barren land and sowing us deep
into my mind and the depth of this unforgettable soil.

Peripeteia (Extract)

… I inspect my thin arms and legs. They have black spots, which I figure are bruises; moreover, my fingers and toes are bleeding from the cuts and scrapes. I notice, under the dim light, marks of cuffs or tight ropes around my wrist. I'm being held captive. The creeping chills through my body. The tightness returns to my chest; trembling, I kneel to the frosty ground. I hear screeching from behind those trees. I shoot my eyes across the barren land to find nothing. I start counting slowly under my breath to calm my pumping heart. My eyes fix on the moonlit soil as I console myself by believing it was just a mere hallucination. My eyes make out a stretched shadow of a moving human figure. I tear up as my body tightens. I feel a heavy breathing down my neck. A crisp and harsh breathing. And as I turn around to face the figure, it lets out a shrieking wail – I jolt up, screaming, pushing the covers and pillows away, holding myself, with tears streaming endlessly down my face…

BIOGRAPHIES

AISHA BORJA – Aisha is a young poet who took part in the Rathbones Folio Mentorships programme in 2018–19. Since Aisha's time as a Rathbones mentee she has left school and become a university student in London where she and Francesca Beard spent time writing, editing and rehearsing poems. Aisha has carried on writing not only for her English Literature and Creative Writing degree but also for herself, as poetry is one of the main things that pulled her through her time locked in her house because of Covid-19. She hopes when things are safe again she will be able to start doing spoken word for a physical audience just like Francesca.

ALICE IMPEY – I am currently studying Art, Music and Performing Arts at college, and I hope to go on to study Paramedic Science at university. My goal is to train to become a paramedic but I would also love to explore careers in the entertainment business, such as acting, motivational speaking and music.

HENNA RAVJIBHAI – When I stepped onto the stage at the First Story Young Writers Festival in 2017 to read a poem about my writing journey, I remember thinking that I had accomplished so much in such a small amount of time. Little did I know that it was just the beginning of an exciting venture into the world of creative writing and the media industry.

The Rathbones Mentorship with the brilliant Joe Dunthorne helped me gain confidence in myself and my writing, allowing me to build the foundations of my writing style without the fear of 'not being good enough'. Since then, I have been able to give back to First Story and worked alongside Sophie Crabtree in the National Writing Day #247Challenge. I am now a proud member of the Writing Squad's tenth cohort, gaining a mentorship with Stevie Ronnie. As well as starting my undergraduate degree in

History at the University of Leeds, I have also recently graduated from Beyond Brontës, a six-month TV industry training scheme, where I was mentored by screenwriter Lisa Holdsworth.

It's safe to say that writing has shaped my future in a way that I could never have imagined. Supportive initiatives run by the likes of Rathbones and First Story have enabled me to see my full potential and have supported me even after the schemes ended. I am forever grateful for the experience I have gained already and I can't wait to see where writing will take me in the next five years.

IMARU LEWIS – After his mentorship, Imaru achieved three A levels, then took a gap year. During this time he did some work mentoring and tutoring primary-aged children, and experimented with different types of writing styles, including script and play writing. But he has decided they are not ready for sharing. In 2020 Imaru began his university career and is an English Literature undergraduate at Royal Holloway University in Surrey. Here, he has discovered a new love and talent for Medieval Literature and Translation.

KATIE PARKINSON – I've been writing for about as long as I can remember, largely thanks to my mum. The hour or so she would spend reading to me before bed was always my favourite part of the day growing up, and the life she would bring to those stories is what inspired me to try and create some of my own. For me, art is really a social thing. It's a way of communicating big and complicated feelings. That's why something like this mentorship is so special, and why it's helped me grow so much. It's a chance to share and talk about the things I've created with someone who understands why I do it. It's the kind of experience that sticks with you forever.

MARIA CLARKE – Maria is a writer and lover of languages, travel, photography and history. As a second-year English Literature and

Creative Writing student at Lancaster University, her writing achievements include being the Overall Winner of the First Story National Writing Competition (2016), shortlisted for the IGGY and Litro Young Writers' Prize (2017) and the Sunderland Short Story Award (2018). She enjoys writing short stories and creative non-fiction, and is currently seeking representation for her debut novel. As well as writing, she loves travelling, spending time with her family and exploring new cultures.

MARIAMAH DAVEY – I'm Mariamah (Mar for short) and writing has always been a part of my life, whether it's been stories in my head or short stories I wrote in my notepad. But it has always been there, and having the opportunity to publish, twice now, has been such an amazing experience. It has changed me forever and I hope it will continue.

NIDAA RAOOF – The Rathbones Mentorship has greatly improved my confidence, both as a writer and person. Through it I was able to explore new things, such as short story postcards and theatre, as well as begin a poetry Instagram account @worlds_to_come.

Since the end of the mentorship I have continued working with First Story, joined the Nottingham Young Writers' Group, become a member of the Nottingham City of Literature Youth Advisory Board, and also worked as part of a committee with City Arts to develop a 'Poetry on the go' app. I am currently studying A levels, whilst continuing to develop my writing through workshops and sharing pieces on social media. The mentorship has encouraged me to focus my writing on important topics such as racism, mental health, feminism and climate change.

PRIYA GILL – My name is Priya Gill, and for the longest time I thought that I would just be a poet. However, through my experiences with First Story, and on this mentorship, I have gained invaluable skills and learnt about the most sophisticated techniques.

Before this, I used to unintentionally limit myself to a very unstructured, yet conscious and relatable kind of poetry. This, I think, had a lot to do with my position of Deputy Youth Mayor and the vast array of projects that I have been a part of since. Aside from poetry, I also enjoy scriptwriting, having written a playlet with some rather interesting characters. I hope to broaden my scope further by studying English Language and Creative Writing at uni.

SHAKIRA IRFAN – Since the mentorship with Rathbones Folio, I have been heavily focused on my degree and the responsibilities associated with a career in healthcare. Spare time only ever came in handfuls across the years, but when it did I found myself gravitating towards writing for reflection, sanity and as a means of grounding myself in a very busy world. My experiences led me to pay particular attention to the question 'what does it mean to be human?' and I spent a lot of time listening, understanding and appreciating just how unique people are. By working with the fantastic A.L. Kennedy through the Mentorships programme, I developed the confidence to observe the world through the eyes of characters that were completely detached from my own life. This challenged my ability to write but, importantly, allowed me to develop a deep sense of empathy that I will certainly take forward, both in my degree and my writing.

SOPHIE CRABTREE – Looking back on my treasured Rathbones mentorship, I realise how firmly it formed the foundation for the writer and person I am now. From there, I've not stopped studying, media and language and finding myself agog at their tsunamic effects. The confidence in my voice that came from my time with Evie Wyld has been put to use advocating for causes close to my heart, such as mental health and women's issues, thanks to Female First and Hive South Yorkshire's help and hosting. I've been honing my poetry skills, the writing form I now revert back to most for its mindful and often stilling approach to viewing life. I recently took my first leap into my career as a digital marketing apprentice, a large part of which constantly challenges me to be creative and find or further brand voices. I'm hopeful for where this will take me.

SOUMYA SHRESTHA – My name is Soumya Shrestha and, for me, writing has turned out to be a safe haven since I was a toddler. It has opened up new opportunities such as First Story, which has helped me to be more creative and allow my ideas to flow smoothly in the form of simple words. Other than writing, I am interested in reading and volunteering as it allows me to understand more about myself and those around me. I have volunteered at multiple youth centres and care homes that have provided me with various ideologies and perspectives, which I believe have been crucial in my journey of writing.

VINCENT OTTERBECK – Since taking part in the Rathbones Folio Mentorships Vinnie finished his A levels, took a gap year and is now finishing his first year studying Geography at Queen Mary University of London. Because of Covid he has been living at home mostly with all his younger siblings, trying to be as good as them at skateboarding. Vinnie has not done any creative writing since doing the mentorship.

WERONIKA BARONOWSKA – Since I last worked with Rathbones Folio Mentorships, I have started studying at the University of Lincoln. The course is Creative Writing and Journalism – I'm choosing to continue writing as a future career. I'm proud to say I've started a blog on all kinds of writing I do and was even part of a student news team. I am overjoyed with how my past year has gone and would recommend it to anyone considering university, especially in these difficult times – having a reason to write keeps you going.

MENTEES AND MENTORS

The Rathbones Folio Mentees, 2017–2021:
Adnaan Ali, Aisha Borja, Alice Impey, Henna Ravjibhai, Imaru Lewis, Katie Parkinson, Maria Clark, Mariamah Davey, Naomi Dairo, Nidaa Raoof, Priya Gill, Shakira Irfan, Sophie Crabtree, Soumya Shrestha, Vilcent Otterbeck and Weronika Baronowska.

The Rathbones Folio Mentors, 2017–2021:
Adam Foulds, AL Kennedy, Alice Jolly, Evie Wyld, Francesca Beard, Joe Dunthorne, Kamila Shamsie, Kathryn Maris, Louise Doughty, Lucy Caldwell, Nikesh Shukla, Paul Farley, Rachel Long, Raymond Antrobus, Ross Raisin, and Sharlene Teo.

ACKNOWLEDGEMENTS

Thanks to our funders and pro bono partners:
Amazon Literary Partnership, Arts Council England, Arvon, The British Library, Cockayne Foundation.

First Story Staff:
Katie Waldegrave and William Fiennes: Founders.

Antonia Byatt: Chief Executive.

Charlotte Prendergast: Head of Learning.

Emma Leahy: Programme and Partnerships Manager (London) and Mentorship Programme lead.

Andy Hill: Programme and Partnerships Manager (West Yorkshire).

Jessica Fear: Programme and Partnerships Manager (East Yorkshire).

Pippa Hennessy: Programme and Partnerships Manager (East Midlands).

Deborah Benson: Head of Development.

Lusungu Chikamata: Operations Manager.

Jay Bhadricha: Editorial Content Manager.

Gabrielle Johnson: Communications Manager.

Melissa Rutnagur: Operations Assistant.

Jess Tickell: Mentorship Programme Lead (2018–2021).

Monica Parle: Executive Director (2014–2018).